AF596192

Love Through Time, History And Mystery

A historical, mystical reincarnation...

EDITORIAL PRIMIGENIOS

Short Novel By

Salomón Leroux

Love Through Time, History And Mystery

A historical, mystical reincarnation...

Editorial Primigenios

First edition, Miami, 2022

ISBN: 9798819517970

Publisher: Editorial Primigenios
Miami Florida.
Email: editorialprimigenios@yahoo.com
Website: https://editorialprimigenios.org

Editing and layout: Eduardo René Casanova Ealo

In *Love Through Time, History and Mystery*, the novel, the Coffee Farm *"Los Naranjos"* of the same name is a leitmotif that is not only a setting, but also a protagonist with its flowering coffee trees bathed in dew and fragrances or covered in persistent dust from the ravines blown by the winds, sometimes breeze, sometimes almost tornado; the murmuring waters of sorrows and joys, singing and tears of slaves.

Salomón Leroux provokes us, she conquers us with a colloquial language, without embellishments, in a direct narrative discourse, of course, in which she transposes times and places, with different characters, who could be the same, disrupted by a historical, mystical reincarnation. Leroux is deceitful and makes fun of us in its apparent simplicity, setting traps for us by bringing us a fine wine of recondite essences in a tin vessel, because behind the apparent simplicity there is a motley intricacy of possible readings, leaving in the culture and sensitivity of the reader the final task of interpreting and enjoying the honeys in the depth of the work.

As in the Masonic rite, the symbols are essence, incarnations of feelings and human truths of multiple edges. Los Naranjos is a drop of arsenic covered in honey, the pain of loneliness, uprooting, the brutality of slavery, sex without love and love beyond physical existence, embodying the presence of absence, come to us in this novel in an almost whispered way. Like the maternal breath on the child's wound, who feels all the healing in the world in the mother's breath, Salomón manages to capture us from the beginning and with a gentle breeze pushes the barge of reading until it takes us to the happy port of the end. Without rhetorical fanfare, the teacher that is Leroux gives us a lesson in perseverance with the simplicity of profound truths.

Augusto Lemus Martínez
Las Vegas 2022

Chapter 1

University

October 3, 1987

The student goes in a hurry, he has papers in his left hand with which he beats rhythmically on his thigh, he is extremely thin, that is why he looks taller than he really is, he has blond and straight hair, it falls on his forehead. He walks through the wide area to get to the faculty of architecture. The trees in the garden interweave its branches and form a gloomy tunnel at that hour of the afternoon when the sun goes down. The chilly wind makes the place feel lonelier.

He comes to the closed door, knocks and someone says:

–Come in.

Upon entering he sees the woman with black hair and a beautiful face. She looks up and meets the green eyes of the young man who hands her papers, she begins to read them while she tells him:

–You are early.

–If I interrupt you, I can wait outside.

–No, sit down, I reviewed the names of the team members. How do you pronounce your last name?

–Yuverr

–Yuver?

–Drag a little more Yuverr.

–Is it French? The name too?

–Yes, Jean Joubert

The woman continues reading and the young man in front of the window pretends to look towards the avenue, but he is really contemplating the reflection of the lady's face in the glass and asks:

—Excuse me teacher, how old are you?

She is surprised, but surreptitiously answers:

—What age do I stand for?

—More than twenty-five and less than thirty, but... that does not matter, I think that when you are eighty, you will still be beautiful.

The woman blushes and looks towards the door through which other students enter, to whom she announces:

—The team is complete, there are five in total and Jean is the team leader for being the one who has been most interested in French constructions.

—Teacher, do you think we should bring any materials? — Odalis asks.

—No, the most important thing is that you remember what you have read, this time we will not take anything more than what is necessary, nobody has been there in a long time, and we must walk lightly to be able to move easily, bring something to draw and measure. I will bring the camera to take pictures and record.

—Well, is someone going to guide us?

—No, as they told me, there are still coffee growers in the area, descendants of slaves. Remember that the French fled Haiti in the 19th century and in the first seventy years they built those coffee plantations in the mountainous area in the east of the island, where still live in these towns still speak what they call Patuá French, a mix between the original French and the pronunciation of words with similarities in African languages.

—Yes, we know about that – Clara continues – and about the way in which the plantations organized. They were farms of medium production and with a slave endowment of no more than forty.

—Indeed, I see that you have read. Do not forget that we are not only going to investigate the house and the surrounding areas, but also for those of urban planning it is important that we discover the roads and the distribution of the housing and production buildings. I wish everyone to be punctual: "We leave at 5 in the morning".

Chapter 2

Jean

Carrying the name of his father and grandfather is something that makes him proud. His great-grandfather arrived in the country at the end of the 19th century, involved with the Independentists from Europe. In 1903 he married a creole and they had only one son, whom they also called Jean, and this in turn to his firstborn, the father of the architecture student, who raised his son alone, because his wife decided to emigrate to another country. For years, the young man always wanted to know about her because he only kept photos that his father had, but time passed, and she never gave any signs of her whereabouts.

Studying away from his house was a difficult decision, he was tormenting by the idea of leaving his father alone, but it was his father who encouraged him to follow his dream of being an architect. Since he was a child, he liked to draw and paint buildings, first those in his neighborhood and then anywhere he passed by. The buildings and public spaces of the city have been the subject of his art. He began from an early age to imagine how he would like the new buildings and houses to be, changing his environment has been his challenge. He has always considered himself an artist and continually defends the concept of architecture as one of the fine arts. For him, an architect must do his work in a complete way, a combination of the need, the purpose, the art, and the pleasure of creating something, which will undoubtedly be part of the lives of people, indirectly or directly. He considers architecture to be the art that connects all other arts with life.

Separated from his father, he has focused on achieving success by graduating. His way of conducting projects and his drawing skills is a source of admiration for other students and teachers; they consider that he has a natural talent for architecture, teachers and students want to collaborate with him and on occasions his ideas have been the subject of discussion because of their novelty and difference.

Jean is an admirer of the works of what he considers to be one of the best architects in Hispanic America, the Mexican Ricardo Legorreta. But it is the colonial architecture in Latin America that he is most interested in investigating, and he bases his designs on it, reinventing and recreating the structures of the buildings built during colonization.

He has few friends and spends his time drawing and recreating existing structures, he is enthusiastic about preserving history, but giving it a modern touch. He reads about construction techniques, new materials, and novel structural forms. He only had short relationships with young women from the school, he has never been interested in long relationships. He knows that he is a man that girls consider interesting and handsome, but with a calm character and sure of what he wants. His best friend is his father, with him he talks about things that he would not tell anyone, he knows that he supports him and encourages him to achieve his goals. They have worked a relationship of trust and knowledge of each other. "The old man", as he says, is his most precious treasure, the reason for his admiration for the sacrifice of being a father and mother, and for teaching him that the family is that person who is always with you without caring about anything else. He is proud to carry the Joubert surname.

Jean loses his usual calm when he is near one of the faculty teachers. He follows her with his eyes through the corridors of the university, she is in charge of research on the construction of French coffee plantations in the eastern part of the country, a project in which he has wanted to work since the beginning of his career, and to which he has finally joined, with the illusion of being able to do his thesis on the subject, and also, why not, meet that professor.

Chapter 3

The Professor

The architect is 32 years old; she has worked hard to remain as the only woman who works in the architecture faculty, and specifically in the department that investigates colonial constructions in the coffee zone. She has always been a determined person to fulfill what she sets out to do, she is very independent and not used to consult her personal matters with anyone.

She is the daughter of a White woman with a Black man, so her family is very varied in terms of skin tone, her three brothers are dark-skinned like her father, tall and enviably muscular. Her sister is a beautiful mulatta, with wide hips and prominent breasts, full red lips that highlight her white teeth. She is thin and white skinned, like her mother, with long, wavy black hair, she always wears it loose; she has a wide smile and big eyes that easily give away her emotions. The professor always keeps a firm posture and wears mostly pants, with which she tries to hide her beautiful basketball legs.

She has been impulsive and independent since she was little, while the other girls played with dolls, she read and investigated insects and butterflies. Her father, being a musician, instilled in her a love for all kinds of music, and from the age of four he taught her to play the guitar and popular music; but Spanish classical music for guitar and orchestra is what she always wanted to perform. But then she decided to study architecture and the guitar took a backseat.

As the only woman in the department, everyone calls her the professor, simply, sometimes by her last name: "Rojas", but she prefers teacher, she thinks it keeps her distance from the students, since she is the youngest of the student's professors, to the point that many times they confuse her and think she is just another student.

When she finished her architecture degree, she was engaged to be married and a few months before the wedding, she broke off the engagement, admitting that she was not in love and that she believed that marriage was not something she was prepared for, that, despite seeing her parents married for over 30 years, she didn't know if she ever really wanted to. The men who know her always fear the same fate as her former boyfriend.

Her maternal grandmother was a very Christian woman and took her to a small Pentecostal church near her house since she was a child, they always came early to listen to the choir rehearsals. She read the sheet music of the hymns and learned them to play them later her guitar. When her grandmother fell ill, she prayed to God that the lady would heal. One day, when she returned from school, she found the pastor in the house and the whole family gathered, her grandmother had died, she left the guitar. After about ten years she went back to playing in college, but she never again played the hymns she heard in the small congregation.

In her father's family they are all descendants of slaves brought from Nigeria, in Africa. They are proud of their heritage and their father actively participates with the Yorubas, this may have been a source of conflict with their mother's family, but at home they always learned to respect the thoughts of others, and their grandmother was the most responsible of family harmony, saying that the most important thing was love, that, within the house, neither politics nor religion were discussed.

When they all got together it was another story, because her father was the only one who had married a White woman, and to top it all off another religion. Her brothers had no problems because they were dark like her father, but her mother, her sister and her, looked like milk stains in the middle of a cup of chocolate. They always ended up in a fight because they did not seem to belong to the same family as their cousins.

The professor knows about the Christians and the Yorubas, but she has decided to believe in science, in research, in having her feet on the ground; she finds it hard to believe in the supernatural, in the mystical. She has not known the true love of a couple, men for her are objects of pleasurable use, she does not want ties, she thinks that she will never give in to a feeling that she considers unnecessary, and sometimes an obstacle to achieving her goals of being a woman successful and independent.

Chapter 4

The Trip

October 4, 1987

Manuel, Odalis's father, goes out to the portal with a cup of coffee in his hand and announces that when the professor arrives, they will leave. The man is a peasant with large hands that stand out with the calluses of the hoe. The sun has drawn lines where the sleeve of the shirt ends. His eyes are small and very blue. He has a big belly that when he sits in the Jeep, he gets pink with the rudder. He walks to the car and Jean follows him carrying two heavy backpacks. They see her arriving. The impatient rest rush to the car.

An hour later they are on the highway heading towards the coffee plantations. In the front seat are Odalis and the professor, behind Ernesto and Jean on one side, on the other Clara and Andrés. The rising sun hits the windshield and highlights the profile of the teacher who is having a pleasant chat with the driver. Passing through the first town, they silently see the two kilometers of houses on the sides of the road.

It is a ghostly place with wooden houses and a store where there are horses tied at the entrance. The young people look at the ruins of what could have been a colonial settlement from the time when coffee grew and brought to the mountains by the French revolutionized the mountains with smaller and more modest buildings than the sugar mills, bringing with them trade to the area. They stop and ask two men leaning against the counter if the road to the haciendas is extremely far:

—What farm? There are only ruins and undergrowth.

—We are heading to those ruins.

—Well, follow the stone path at the end of the town, the one that leaves the road, but be careful, it is dangerous. The mules slip and fall, —I do not know if that "*tareco*" (old car) will be able to make it.

Thank you, we will have it in mind.

Few meters further on they see the exit to the causeway. It is a narrow and rocky trail that makes young people have fun with the jumps caused by the bumps in the road. Manuel sits behind the wheel and asks them to be quiet, as they turn the curve, they can see the cliffs that the mountain hides, great cliffs along which the stones roll that jump as the car slowly passes. Jean runs over and places his hand on the teacher's shoulder, who, frightened, squeezes the seat hard.

The journey is slow, and they do it in silence, they do not want to look at the side of the ravine, because the wheels of the car adjust to the edge of the road. They insist on looking to the opposite side, to the mountain that imposes itself with its exuberant vegetation, which insisted on not seeing spaces without weeds. They cannot see the chasm, it is a great wall, which with the humidity of the fog appears an intense olive green. You can see the streams that like silver threads go down between the few rocks. Uphill the fog only allows them to see the lights of the car on the road.

At the top there is a plateau, they stop to see the valley. From this point you can see the red tile roofs cured by the time of the old mansions. Sitting on the edge with his feet dangling into the void, Jean contemplates the place where the moist green of the plants contrasts with the clouds that seem to intersect with the branches of the trees and extends his hand as if to touch them. In the distance the palm trees highlight their majesty among the fruit trees and higher up the orange trees show golden sparkles that shine with the first rays of the sun. At the end, on the other side of the mountains, the coffee plantations flourished.

The young man turns his eyes towards the professor with her back to his, who is trying to pick up her hair blown by the wind. Aware that he is watching her, she moves slowly and covers the back of her neck, causing the young man to get up from her and approach her, asking if she is cold.

—No, but the wind ruffles my hair.

—If you want, I will lend you my jacket, the air is freezing.

—It is the climate of these mountains. The sun does not heat the earth, there is vegetation.

—Anyway, take it.

The young man places his jacket on the shoulders of the woman who for a moment feels the heat of proximity and shudders.

They continue the journey along the path that becomes narrower and narrower and surrounded by bushy cedars, they can no longer see the sky. The weather is getting colder, and the vegetation begins to be woody. They slide across a carpet of fallen leaves. In the end, the *batey*. They are receiving by children who play with the cane of a gray-haired Black man who smokes tobacco sitting on a stool. They ask:

—Sir, how do we get to Los Naranjos?

—Who goes to Los Naranjos? What are you going to do? You could not get there into that car. You must continue foot.

The Black man looks annoyed, takes the cane, and swings it like a sword trying to keep the visitors away. He looks his is in his nineties, but is over a hundred, still stocky and slightly stooped, with frizzy white hair. He gets up and shouts into the "*bohío*" with unintelligible words. The professor gets out of the car and asks the old man if anyone lives in the house on the coffee plantation. A dark woman comes out and answers:

—Nobody lives there, the old man has the keys, but he does not give them.

—We are investigating the architecture of French mansions and we want to take photos and make notes — says the teacher.

—Well, I cannot, says the upset old man and sits back on the stool.

—Jean from the car listens and sees the nervous and contradictory gesture reflected in the face of the teacher, she gets out and faces the old man.

—Look sir, we are not going to do any harm; we are students, and we want to investigate this construction.

The Black man looks at him with open eyes, as if he were seeing an apparition. Then he looks at the brown-haired person and puts his hand on his head, stands up reverently and says:

—"Mesieh".

Pulling keys out of his pocket he hands them to her and begins to say things in what appears to be Patoan French. The Black woman calls the children, and they enter the hut. The Black old man follows her scratching his head. The young people begin to call Jean “Mesié” and, laughing, they bow.

They climb the path full of mosses and ferns that leads to Los Naranjos. It is the hour of sunset. It begins to get dark quickly and they hurry because they fear they will not reach the ruins before nightfall. The road is uncomfortable and wet, they continually slip. They walk along the path as if carrying soaps in their shoes. Jean notices that the teacher is tired. The other young men help the girls, and he approaches her and taking the woman's waist, he draws her towards him. She lets herself go and leaning her body against the young man's, letting him almost carry her uphill.

It is the first time that the bodies are stuck to each other, and at that moment the young man would like that unpleasant and rugged path to be eternal. He does not think about his wet and tired feet, nor the darkness. He only feels his arm around his waist. He knows she is trying not to continually lean on his side, but he keeps her pressed against him without letting her touch the floor. She feels the beating of the young man's heart while her own is racing.

They pass through the ruins of the entrance where two ruined iron doors recall the splendor of the place where the former owners lived. When they arrive it is completely dark, they turn on their flashlights to discover an entrance and settle in at least for that night, they have not eaten anything, but fatigue only makes them want a place to lie down and spend the night. They have not been able to upload the rest of the things, only the personal backpacks. The only lights are the flashlights, and it is necessary to save the batteries. They decide to try to sleep.

Chapter 5

Los Naranjos

October 5, 1987

The crowing of a rooster wakes up Jean who looks at his watch, it is four in the morning. Everything is dark, but he knows that she sleeps opposite. He strains but cannot see past his feet on the backpack. She turns on a flashlight and looks for something on the floor. He approaches her and when he speaks to her, she turns:

—It is me, what is going on?

I do not see, and I cannot find the glasses box.

—"Here it is," he says as he picks up the case and hands it to her.

Noticing that the woman does not see him, he takes her hand. She thanks him, puts on her glasses, and watches him kneeling and staring at her. Their faces are close, and they can exchange breath, she steps back and turns off the light. Jean returns to his corner and notices that the rooster has not screwed again.

Few hours later, after breakfast, the teacher sits at the top of the front steps from where she sees the ruins of the entrance to the courtyard of the hacienda, the terrace, what used to be the garden, and the ruins of the so-called "quartier where the slaves slept. In the center are the ruins of the fountain and the pond where there are ducks, behind them the doors of the house of the owners of the coffee plantation, built on the warehouse where they kept the coffee.

The mansion, as the slaves called it, is a stone construction with cedar columns at each corner of the rectangle and in the middle of the longitudinal parts. It has two floors, the first about five meters high where the stored coffee with two large doors through which the carts entered with the product to be store. The second floor, reached by a wide limestone staircase leading to the wide corridor, is the mansion. A balcony runs along all four sides with an iron railing that is sometimes missing. Two cedar doors and windows with French shutters on the leaves appear on the main facade and three other small doors on the rest, on the opposite side of the main entrance another wooden staircase, of which only few steps are still.

The teacher standing at the top of the stairs explains:

—If you look closely, you will notice the difference with the Spanish constructions, here the rectangle has been incredibly careful. The sashes of the windows must have been shutter style, there are still around, which will give us an idea of the dimensions. The cedar tejamil, as they called the roof tiles, we must try to collect them and take them to make replicas, in case one day we want to rebuild here.

—They really built the houses of the landowners in a strategic place, from where they can see entire plantation – Clara comments.

—Certainly, from where we are, the portal, we can see the guardrail that leads to the other parts, and where the stone tower is, it must be where the bell was to call the activities, that on the sides must have been the barracks of the slaves

– Andrés clarifies.

—Everything we have read is helping us, the teacher was right, we could not come until we had studied everything – emphasizes Odalis.

—We will work in three research groups: Odalis and Ernesto the dryers, Clara and Andrés, the garden, and the barracks. Jean and I, the house.

—Finally, the teacher summarizes: "Like most coffee settlements, Los Naranjos is in a mountainous valley, with slopes of up to twenty-five percent. The river runs along the side between the hacienda and the coffee plantations. Water was a key part in the development of production and the life of the "batey." The other fundamental thing was the production cycle, which with the habitable areas made up an integrated area, where the productive sequence, the aqueduct, the pools, the coffee house, the fermentation tanks, and the dryers were related. Keep in mind that the two-story house kept its stone walls, the coffee drying rooms in the form of terraces, the circular mill moved by horses called the "tahona," the warehouse, where crockery, and punishment instruments such as stocks and shackles were storage.

Chapter 6

Teamwork

October 6, 1987

Odalis and Ernesto go to the dryers, which is the area farthest from the house. Everything seems to show that the peasants of the area still use the place. Once again, they see the Black man smoking in the shack and watching his steps. This couple has fun and takes advantage of the trip to organize their wedding. They have known each other since high school and have been dating for years until they decided to get married to finish their last year of college. She has always wanted to be the leader in everything, and he only thinks of pleasing her, that is why in the middle of her investigation he lets himself carried away by her, although sometimes he does not agree with the ideas she raises.

They ask the Black man how to get to the dryers and the fermentation tanks. This shows an old path that runs behind the slave barracks, walking along the side of the mountain and following the course of the river. Upon reaching the place, you can see the rectangles built on the sloping floor with walls approximately 3.5 centimeters high where the collected coffee poured to dry. The patio is grassy, fruit and flower bushes have grown, and the paths along which the carts passed have disappeared. The young people try to make their way through the undergrowth to be able to measure and take pictures.

—I do not know why the teacher did not let Jean be in another team with you or with Clara, I do not see the need for her to work with the most advanced student when she can help the others on the team, don't you think, Ernesto?

—I was thinking about that, he has knowledge and is working for his thesis and needs information, which is why she wants to work closer to him.

—I do not know; I sec a strange movement with those.

—Do not be mean, she is a particularly good teacher, and she sure wants to help him.

—But he looks for her and is aware of everything, even when she is unprotected like the other day, he gave her his jacket.

—Hey, you women do not let one be gentlemanly, you always think what is not.

—Do not start with the same thing that I am always sending you.

—It is not that, just...

—Okay, let us go to work because we do not have all day for that, and you know it rains here every day.

In the garden, Andrés and Clara try to clean what still is of the limestone fountain. It was a rose whose center sprouted the water that when recycled fell on the circle that forms the pond. The fountain is the crucial point from which the axes that define the octagonal shape of the garden appear, delimited by the buildings that make up the hacienda and the planimetric composition of The Batey, where sometimes the surface flattened. When looking at the mansion from the garden, you can appreciate the harmony between the architecture and the landscape of the place, the adaptation to the topography, which you can perfectly see when taking the photos.

From the garden you can see the buildings of the hacienda, the mansion that is one level higher than the others, the barracks, the foreman's house, and the kitchen, which was strategically were the winds would not contaminate the coffee. with the smell of food, in this case it is on the slope of the hill near the mansion, and far from the dryers.

On one side is the mill to remove the straw from the coffee, you can only see lines that show its circular shape, the mud has covered the central part. The young clean the ferns and bushes that grow around them. Everything is wet. Drops of rain begin to fall, and the water accumulates and forms a gelatinous slime that is difficult to move through.

They run towards the mansion where they find their companions who are also looking to protect themselves from the rain that falls in torrents. The afternoon has turned black, and the sound of lightning is frightening. Lightning is the only light that enters through the cracks in the door. They are all wet. The women move to a corner with the intention of changing their clothes, the young men go to the opposite place. At alternate times, the place lights up and darkens, the eyes of the young people lost trying to guess the figure of the young women. Jean stunned to see the teacher's half naked body. She knows that Jean is looking at her.

When the rain stops it is still early, it is the second night and they have toured part of the settlement, they have seen the mansion in the sunlight, the quartiers, the garden, the dryer, the fountain, and the green mountains around the esplanade. The afternoon is falling, and the sun is going down behind the mountains. The teacher sits on the steps, guitar in hand, and begins to play a sad melody. The young men come out with a bottle of rum and glasses.

—Teacher — says Odalis — why that sadness? No, no, no, you must be happy, look, have a drink, and warm up.

—"Yes, teacher, we are going to sing, I know she likes Spanish songs," Ernesto says as he sits next to the woman with the guitar.

—If he comes, let us go with the "Mocedades," the one they sang in the amphitheater on the day of the student gala, Clara says and begins to sing: "A seagull without feathers...," the others sing too.

Jean, who remained inside the house, goes out and sits on the wall that makes an angle with the steps from where she can see the teacher while she plays the guitar, she lowers her head and pretends to look at the chords she places with her left hand. They continue singing and drinking the rum from the bottle until the place goes dark, there is only one lamp burning inside the house and they are under the light of the stars and a dim moon partially covered by few clouds that move slowly.

The rest of the young people have entered, and Jean and the teacher remain, she is playing her sad music again.

—Why do you play something so sad?

—It is a Spanish ballad, although it seems sad, it is not. It is call "Historia de Amor," and in its melody you can appreciate the tenderness of affection that describe, if you listen carefully, you will realize it.

The young man leans against the railing and closes his eyes, she continues to play, now her fingers run over the strings, and she looks at him, she can see him without fear of him returning her gaze, his large receding hairline makes him look older. They make him look older than the rest of the young. She sees his closed eyes and the stillness with which he listens to the notes. She feels confused and strange because the age difference is always present in her mind and that she is a professional, who would not allow a young student to make a mistake and compromise her work in college. Still, she keeps looking at him.

Chapter 7

Odalis and Ernesto

There is no one who knows Odalis who has not always related her to Ernesto, they did primary, secondary and preschool together. When deciding to study at university, she wanted to be an architect, he wanted to go abroad to study because he is fascinated by computers. After confrontations, he relented, and they went to study what she wanted.

They are always together, the same classes, the same projects, they are one person. There are times, he does not speak, she says what he thinks, and what he does not think, but he nods. She organizes everything, whether they go to her parents' house for the weekend, whether they see a movie, or whether they eat spaghetti every Sunday. The shirts, the pants, the hairstyle, if not the black shoe, or the blue belt, which she matches with the shirt. "Do not eat butter you get fat, look at the belly that is growing out of you"

—But I like it, a little for bread and coffee with milk.

—Well, put a little in the cup and that way when you wet the bread with coffee it will taste the same.

—You are crazy, it does not taste the same.

Try it and see, look at this is what you should do she inserts a teaspoon of butter in the young man's milk.

—But... leave that, it is my latte... you have already ruined it.

—You eat it because you are not going to waste the milk, look how expensive it is.

This is how they spend time, with different ideas and opposing opinions. They have a room for the two of them in the student dormitories, and the others see them as a married couple. They are in their last year, like Jean, and they have known each other for a long time, it can say that they are good friends. Everyone is interested in the coffee plantation project.

In the last month Odalis has been insisting on the trip to Los Naranjos, because she knows that it is a difficult trip, in a mountainous area that requires good physical preparation, and now that she is pregnant, she wants to be sure that the pregnancy does not prevent her from taking part in the project.

Ernesto is very worried because he did not plan to have a family so quickly, and the pregnancy took him by surprise, but Odalis is the love of his life and having a child with her is something that fills him with joy, and illusion. He knows that for her the coffee plantation project is important, for him, it is something else to do in his career, he is determined to finish architecture and start with computer engineering, which he has always wanted to study. He worries because he is going to have to work and study at the same time, and with the baby things are going to get complicated for him.

Odalis's family has planned everything, in a month it will be her wedding, and after they graduate, they will live in her parents' house. The only thing that counts is her mother, a woman who has worked tirelessly so that her only child went to college. She works long hours in a factory and lives in a humble house that she keeps extremely organized and clean. Ernesto's mother and future wife are similar in character, which is why sometimes the most banal topics can become the discussion of the night when the in-laws talk.

—Ernesto's suit is going to be white, with a purple bow. I saw it in a fashion magazine, and I loved it.

—Do you think that with that belly he should wear a white suit? Also, white is for the bride.

—Who says that? Men also dress in white, it is their first and only wedding too, because, God forbid, but if they get divorced, they may not marry again.

—Do not be a bird of ill omen, shut up that mouth.

It is a saying...

—You better find another suit, since Odalis is wearing white.

—No, the one in the magazine is particularly good for him.

—Then let him start exercising and go on a diet to lose his belly.

—No way, you cannot even mention it, he will stop eating and will become anemic.

All night women arguing and young men trying to watch a movie. Ernesto imagines what married life will be like living with his in-laws and the arguments when his mother comes to visit them. But, in the end, he considers all this part of the happiness he wants to have in his married life. Fortunately, his father-in-law hardly speaks and when they go out on the patio, they can have their beers in peace.

Chapter 8

Clara

She is the youngest of the group, and the shyest, she is always quiet and lost in her thoughts, which no one can figure out. She has a knack for building models, and everyone looks for her when it comes to her. In the first years of her degree, she made few friends, including Odalis and Ernesto, who, being only a year older than her, treat her like a little sister, one of those who are born when we are already teenagers, and we believe they are our daughters. The young woman lives with her parents and is the only daughter, they fought hard to have children since her youth, but they only managed a single pregnancy, that is why they have pampered her and surrounded her with everything a young woman could wish for, but the father has become ill with prostate cancer and the lady has devoted herself body and soul to the care of her husband.

Clara and Odalis are best friends, who borrow their clothes and spend time together in the room gossiping and laughing. Ernesto often must buy the same things for both because they lend each other anything and, in the end, they do not know those to whom that belongs. When they go to parties, they always look for a friend, to see if they can get a boyfriend for her, but so far not even with glue, nothing at all. She is very childish, she is stuck in adolescence, she still paints little dolls in her notebooks.

She decided to study architecture because her father always wanted to do it, but he never had the opportunity because it is an expensive career and he never had the means, so he raised the money since Clara was born so that she could go to university. She feels committed and overwhelmed because, although she has a knack for design and the teachers consider that she has a good future as a professional, she would have wanted to study sculpture, she is always drawing the pieces she wants to create, and in her room, she has thousands of minifigures that has made of clay. She is excited about finishing and showing her title to her father and then being able to dedicate herself to what she most desires: sculpting.

Few days before the trip, the doctors informed the family that the man is terribly ill and that they fear that he will not have longer to live. She adores her parents and knows that her mother would die of pain with the absence of her partner for so long, the man who has given everything for them. Before leaving, she promised her father that she would finish her degree and bring her degree so that she could hang it in a place where she could see it continuously and be proud of her.

Clara uploads a photo of the family where she, her mother and her father are, in which she thinks continuously, she is afraid that he will die before seeing her graduate, which is why she insists on doing the best she can. She can finish on time; She has given up her desire to sculpt to understand architecture and the trip to the coffee plantation can help her in her desire to draft a good thesis that will allow her to finish her degree without problems. But since she always carries with her, her sketchbook where she draws her ideas for her tiny sculptural ones, the ones she has filled her room and her whole house with.

She has been making tiny sculptures since she was little when she played with plasticine in the children's circle. The teacher noticed that she always, unlike the other children, when she made the dolls, she made them small and with detail, she could make a whole family of little animals with little material; so, she was interested in letting the girl develop her vocation. Since then, she has made millions of little figurines, of everything, carts, houses, trees, people, in short, when someone needs help for a model, she is there to put into practice what she likes the most.

Chapter 9

Andrew

Young Andrés does not know who he really is, his mother is a teacher, and his father is a lawyer, they were never at home, and he stayed in the care of the babysitter, a fat and smiling lady who prepared dulce de leche for him to drink calcium because he did not like plain milk. She taught him to cook and make desserts, they spent hours together, and his childhood games played in the kitchen of the house where she kept him company between chores.

He studied architecture because his father always said that: "No one lives from the kitchen, and who knows if you are going to be good" and since he also likes drawing, he thought that at least doing something that would please his father and not be so heavy. His mother has always supported him in everything, he and his sister have always been the pride of the lady, because they both finished high school and the girl studied medicine and he is also a professional who is doing very well, because his designs are always novel.

The only concern of his parents is that Andrés shows no intention of starting a family, and since he is the son, he is the one who can pass on the surname to the new generations. As his father says: When are you going to introduce me to the future mother of my grandchildren?

—Dad, always with the same thing, I already told you that someday I will bring you someone, for now I am focusing on my new business.

—But architecture is not enough for you, I do not know if that idea of yours to cook in front of people will work, you know that kitchens are always out of reach for diners.

—Precisely that is the idea that they see that what cooked is fresh and they can see the chef in action.

—I do not know...

—Mijo and the girl you were dating, are you never going to bring her?

—Mom is a coworker, she is not my girlfriend, we only go out to distract ourselves.

—But who knows sometimes that's how love is born?

—Mijo, is that the unattractive you mentioned to me?

—Yes, dad, but I am telling you, she is not my girlfriend.

—Well, the unattractive come out faithful.

—Who says? The one who is going to be faithful is, even if she is pretty, and the one who is not, she is not.

—That is true, look, your mom has always been faithful to me.

—Yes, but I cannot say the same about you.

—Old you know that you have been my only love.

—Your only love is possible, but the only one in your bed I do not know.

—Come, that is why I have not been married or engaged, there is no way to be single and free.

—Andresito, but it is time for you to settle down and have your family, look at how well your sister has done, and now she is already pregnant for the second time.

—Yes, mom, but that is different, she has always wanted to have a family and children, but you know that I have my doubts, and now with this restaurant thing, I do not have enough time to do more than work.

—Look *mijo*, in life there is time for everything. I would like to meet your children and spend time with them. our sister is younger, and she already has a family.

—I know mom, I promise you I will think about it, and I will do that, I say find a girlfriend first. Don't you think?

Conversations like this would take place in the coming years for Andrés and his parents, not knowing that fate had surprises in store for the young man.

Chapter 10

The History

Los Naranjos, October 18, 1857.

The young Frenchman walks from one side of the portal to the other, he wears riding boots and spurs that sound on the stones, in his left hand he holds a whip with which he rhythmically hits his thigh. He continually looks at the gate.

—Do not be impatient, the journey is long, and the women carry things. Here comes a Black man running – says the priest – surely, he brings news.

—Oui, he is coming to the maison.

—Another Black slave yells: "the mules are coming," "they are coming for the spring"

The young man rushes to the spring, the slaves see him run and laugh.

The priest and the old Black person contemplate the garden. It is late afternoon and the sun hides behind the mountains and its last rays redden the sky. The smell of jasmine invades the environment, and the song of the crickets is still faint. From the garden you can see the house lit by large lamps and candles. Its masonry walls, damp due to the continuous rain of the place, allow the ferns to grow and give it a stately appearance. Everything is peaceful and picturesque at this hour. The batey is celebrating, the moon illuminates the entire garden where the young couple approach the house with their arms around each other. They kiss repeatedly and the young man takes her to the lily pads. From the quartier comes the sound of the slaves who sing while drinking liquor that the master distributed to celebrate the arrival of his mother and wife.

Madame Joubert gazes at the painting of her husband leaning his head against her frame. The young blond man rejects the cup of coffee that his wife offers him and goes to hug his mother.

—Son, let us go to France or Spain if you want. What need do we have of these coffee plantations?

—I was born in these coffee plantations. In Europe, today you are a noble and tomorrow a beheaded.

—Please— Carmen interrupts them— Look at the moon, it is beautiful.

—Yes mother, see the garden in the moonlight.

—No, go, I am fine here.

Father Nataniel approaches and asks:

—Happy, my daughter?

—Yes, finally with my husband. I was so afraid that he would seek solace in a Creole.

—Do not think that. He only loves you.

—But I am ten years older and Spanish. Besides, there are things that I am not going to be able to give him.

—Do not worry, God sends children.

—God hear you father, because we have tried, and nothing works for us.

—Look here, the women of the slaves know about herbs and remedies for fertility, perhaps when you get to know them better, one of them will help you.

—Those things scare me. How effective can these concoctions made by the slaves be?

—They know natural medicine, remember that in Africa they have been healing with plants for thousands of years.

Chapter 11

The Miracle

January 19, 1858. Los Naranjos

Several months have passed and Jean is happy in the company of his wife who is happier every day to live in the coffee plantation, for her Los Naranjos is a paradise in which her husband goes out of his way to please her, he has ordered to bring many luxurious things from the capital, and has bought her a Steinway & Son piano, one of the most expensive for her to fill the afternoons with her music. She has not achieved her longed-for pregnancy and that saddens her, she has thought about it and has decided to call the black Joaquina to tell her how to contact the village healer, this Justa, they say she works miracles with herbs.

—But ma'am. How are we going to see that sorcerer?

—I have already dealt with everything Joaquina, it is the only thing left for me to deal with, what —I want most is to give my dear Jean a child.

—And did you want me to go with you without anyone knowing about it? That seems dangerous to me.

—We will say that we are going to the town to buy fabrics.

—You will not believe it, look at everything that the Lord has ordered for you, you can set up your own store.

—We will find an excuse, but today we are going to see that woman, Justa.

Determined and accompanied by Joaquina, they secretly leave the hacienda in a caleza, (a horse drawn carriage). They go to the town. The coachman, a Black man, had obtained the address of the house of the woman who dedicated to making the so-called miracles. The Spaniard is nervous but determined to find a solution. The Black woman prays the rosary. She is very afraid of witchcraft, she knows that Africans know strange things, but she was raising by French colonizers and taught to pray and trust in the Divine.

Finally, they arrive at the shack on the outskirts of town. It is late afternoon and cloudy. It looks like rain is going to fall, they go in and sit on stools while a Black man offers them something to drink that they do not accept.

—The healer will attend you now; she is preparing a medicine that she says is for you.

—But if we have not talked to her, how can she know what she is going to give my lady?

—She knows what people need before they come.

—Madam, this scares me, it looks like witchcraft.

—Do not worry, Joaquina, we are here, and everything will be fine.

An hour later, Justa comes out with a vial in her hands:

—Look Dona, this is the medicine you need; she should take it only on the day she is going to have sex with her husband, it is dangerous for her to take it if she is not going to sleep with him.

—But how will she know that he is going to look for her?

—Well, she must know the customs that he has and the signs that he gives her when he wants to be with her. If you remember, do not take it if she is not going to be with him.

—Do not worry, I will follow the request.

—"What if she takes it and he doesn't come over?"

—It is dangerous, it can create worse evils for her.

Back at the mansion, Joaquina follows her prayers, Carmen wants to put medicine into practice and only wants to get there to prepare the bedroom so that Jean wants her that night. It is raining, the carriage is going slowly because there is already mud and the path to Los Naranjos is dangerous. The Spanish woman thinks that when she arrives, Jean will be already in the bed waiting for her, without thinking, she opens the bottle and takes a little of her drink.

—But ma'am, what had you done? We have not arrived at the house yet, what if the man does not look for her today?

—"I managed to wheedle it out," she says with a mischievous smile on her lips.

Unexpectedly the carriage stops abruptly, sways and tilts.

—Slave, what was that? — asks Joaquina.

—Black, our axle broke, and a wheel came off, do not move because with the tilt it can turn, do not worry, I am going to walk to the hacienda to get help.

—Oh God, now what are we going to do with you madame?

—Calm down Joaquina, they will surely come to help us.

The rain continues to fall, and the quiet women try not to move inside the *caleza*, more than two hours have passed, and no one has arrived, it is midnight, the woman feels dizzy and leans her head on the Black woman's shoulder and falls asleep. Finally, the coachman appears with other slaves and the master.

—How did it occur to you to go out with the storm that was coming? I was very worried, nobody knew where you were, and this Black woman who does not think, where did you go?

—Do not claim her master, it is my fault. I distracted her on the way back from passing by where my cousin was, the one who sells African clothes.

—Slave you know they cannot go out without me knowing. Look how the lady is, she is burning with fever.

—I am sorry, it is my fault, let us go so I can prepare something hot for her and change her wet clothes.

They quickly put the woman on a stretcher and two slaves take her to the house, the woman is unconscious. Joaquina goes to the kitchen and prepares a garlic and ginger tea, and she goes upstairs with another Black woman who carries hot water to put warm clothes on the lady. They spend the whole night looking for a way to lower the fever in the lady, finally at dawn she is asleep, and temperature is normal. The symptoms have disappeared when the remedy she took has expired in her body, the Black woman prays by the bedside of her beloved lady and looks at the bottle, then she takes it with the intention of throwing it away, but the lady stops her.

—No Joaquina, leave it there, I assure you that next time I will be more careful.

Chapter 12

Life and Death

October 25, 1859. The Orange Trees

Madame Joubert, kneeling before the image of the crucified Christ, prays between sobs for Carmen. They have already sent a Black man for the doctor, but it is raining, and the mules cannot get through, the slave left two days ago. The slave who helps her has only given birth twice. Jean hits the hallway wall and cries, his shirt is open, and he sweats, the drops run down his body, and he only thinks of his wife's moans. The priest kneeling on small stones in a corner has been praying all day. In the "quartier," Black people perform rituals invoking African gods. Everyone awaits the birth. Through the garden the shadows pass confused between the wind and the rain, they bet between life and death.

The Black women run with hot water and clothes, the hours pass, and the light of dawn begins to climb the eastern hills. The baby has just been born. Joaquina picks him up and shouts: "My master is a little boy, a little boy." Jean enters the room and without looking at the child runs to where Carmen is asleep, her breathing is terribly slow. She is exhausted. The man kneels in front of his wife's bed and takes her hands, looks at the crucifix and exclaims: "My life for hers", "Take the child, but not her". The doctor enters the room. It is dawn and a cold mist enters through the window. Carmen is dead.

Chapter 13

Fire!

The Orange Trees, April 19, 1860

Jean drinks from the bottle of rum that has been his only company since Carmen's death. He does not know anything about the boy. Madame Joubert suffers and occupies her time weaving and wishing to return to France. Six months have passed and the young man paints and tears up a picture of his wife every day, he is obsessed with recreating Carmen's smile. The slave Joaquina breastfeeds the child and sings:

Do, do piti, die
Do, do piti, die
do, do, domi
do, do, domi
Do, do, piti, die
oh my
O, wi, do, me

The desperate Jean goes out and lost in the dense bushes that surround the coffee plantation. Few hours later the priest looks at the coffee plantation waiting for him to return and becomes anguished; he knows that sometimes he goes away for days.

The smell of coffee drying is strong in the air, and the Black women clean the wooden floor. The dogs are loose, and the overseers shoot at anything that moves.

—Do not worry father, the young man knows the trails by heart, we already sent a slave to look for him, do not be impatient. The madam cries if she does not know about him.

They have spent the entire day waiting for the man to return, suddenly a Black man appears shouting: "Fire, there is fire in the coffee plantation." Everyone runs, but it is useless, there is no way to enter. The flames are devouring everything. Madame Joubert cries inconsolably, crying out for her son who rides his steed through the flames with a torch in hand. Chaos reigns and the priest falls in and cries out to God. In the quartier the Black women shout and throw water on the walls because the heat of the fire arrives looking like it is going to catch them too. The rancher has disappeared engulfed in flames and the desperate scream of the horse comes as a last attempt to survive.

In the morning the smell of burning still invades the atmosphere and the rain falls forming a thick black mud, the slaves look for remains of the young man and his horse, but only part of the mount had recovered, it is impossible to discover anything else between the la rot and pestilence. There is nothing left on the hill where the coffee crop flourished, only the black mountain that would never regain its splendor.

Few days later, Father Nataniel recites a mass in front of an empty tomb. Jean's body has not found. The rain falls. Everyone rushes to the house and takes refuge in the heat of the burning water that warms their bodies.

—Father, I have decided to sell Los Naranjos — says Madame Joubert.

—Think about it, you can leave an administrator, —Los Naranjos are the heritage of young Jean.

—No, he goes to France with me, and he will never return to this land.

—It is the land of his father and now his.

—This land has only brought misfortune to my family, first my beloved husband, then Carmen and now my son. No, I am taking my grandson, who will not know the existence of this place.

Chapter 14

Paris

Summer of 1889

The midday sun cuts the raindrops on the sidewalk, everyone walks to the magnificent exhibition. The young assistant of Monsieur Eiffel tries to reach the tower and rushes to cross the bridge over the Seine, he has worked tirelessly on the construction of the tower designed for the contest of the Universal Exhibition of 1889, held in Paris on the centenary of the French revolution. More than seven hundred projects presented, but none could develop with a similar height, an achievement achieved by Maurice Koechlin, another assistant to the architect Eiffel, who was inspire by the study of the femur bone for the design of the tower. He discovered that the internal structure, narrow in the middle and expanded at the ends, saved materials, and gave greater strength and flexibility.

The young engineer is proud of his participation in the work, even if it was little, since the project needed more than fifty designers and engineers, who produced more than 5,300–part designs, mainly because of his work with the architect Stephen Sauvestre, who designed the final look of the tower. At first artists, intellectuals and architects criticized Gustave's work, pointing out that the tower was "an iron monster" that spoiled the aesthetics of the city, but for Jean it is the best thing that has built in Paris, and he knows that over time everyone will see her as a great symbol. He has worked through the years, two months, and five days of construction to achieve the magical moment when the tower lit up green on the night of December 12 with electricity generated from vegetable oil.

Young Jean's friends from Spain have arrived with the envoy from America who brings news of the revolution on the Island. This envoy is a very eloquent poet, a dreamer, free-thinking like those who frequent the Rue de Rivoli. Everything related to the island is news of interest to the young engineer, the Black woman who has taken care of him since his mother died has told him things about the Caribbean, its smells, its fields, the drum, the sun, the beach, and the coffee plantation. His Spanish cousins do nothing but talk about "mulato" women and rum, tobacco and this poet who improvises simple love verses for them. He today he will meet him, and he will know when the trip is.

From the tower Javier sees his cousin approaching wet from the drizzle and almost running between the umbrellas and tells:

–Jean joined the movement when he was a student, and his grandmother suspended all monetary aid forbidding to mention his name.

–He continued studying with the help of Monsieur Eiffel. Look, it is that one, the one who walks dancing and hits his thigh with the cane.

Jean finally approaches and greets the man in the black frock coat as they continue their ascent of the tower. From the tower they contemplate the city, a 360° view, in the distance they see the Sacre Coeur, the golden dome of Les Invalides, Notre Dame Cathedral, the Trocadero gardens, Fine Arts, and the Seine River that runs between magnificent residential buildings.

After a while, as they walk away, the poet stares at the flag of the Republic on the tower and asks:

–How tall is the tower?

—Three hundred and thirty meters. It is the tallest tower in the world, he says proudly.

—The truth is that it still seems taller

—It is the illusion of perspective from the ground.

They arrive at Rue Rivoli, and it is getting dark. In the small bar, a man plays the accordion to the songs of Debussy, which is the fashion in the streets of Paris. They invite the young poet to read his poems in French. Jean dreams of his arrival on the island and a tear runs down his cheek and he drink. He drinks the cognac of farewell, of goodbye to his beloved Paris.

It is his last day in the city where he has lived for more than twenty years, and now he faces a new life in a country that, although he was born in, he does not remember. He rushes to the house where his grandmother and the black Joaquina who has been his surrogate mother live. He knocks on the huge door, and the Black woman opens and hugs him:

—Jean, my Jean, you have finally decided to return home. Your grandmother will be happy to see you, she does nothing but ask if you have come.

—Not my dear, I just came to say goodbye because tomorrow I leave for the island.

—That cannot be, you know that there is nothing left there, that everything lost, and your grandmother would die if she knew.

—I just want to say goodbye to her. I would not want to leave without saying goodbye, besides, I would like to know where my parents' graves are.

—I do not know son, she does not want to give information about that, I only remember that the farm called Los Naranjos.

Madame Joubert enters, and she hastens to embrace the young man:

—My beloved Jean you have returned, look how thin you are, and those clothes, where did you get them? You look like a community member; Joaquina takes out one of the young man's suits and lets him take a bath. You must prepare the chicken that he likes and the toast, even if it is in the afternoon.

—No grandma, I came to say goodbye, tomorrow I leave for the island.

—To the island? You are crazy, there you can only find death. they are at war against the Spanish, they do not want the settlers there anymore.

—That is why I am going to meet with the revolutionaries to achieve the independence of the island.

—Who put these ideas in your head? You do not need to go back there; you do not even speak Spanish well. Surely, you have gotten together with those rioters from the commune.

—Grandma, I want to know where the graves of my parents are.

—Never, in that place there is only death, do not think that I am going to let you use your father's fortune for that madness.

—I do not want money I just want to know where they are.

—I do not know, your grandfather knew the location, and the last news we had before his death was that the Black people had revolted against the whites in '68, and ranchers left the island.

—But documents must remain.

—There is nothing left, everything was there in the foreman's house.

—But do you at least remember the area where is it?

—In the East, I only remember that more than twenty years have passed, and we never mention it again.

—Well, I must go, they must be waiting for me.

Jean thinks better of things, here you have everything, there is your family and Joaquina who has been like your mother, if you leave now, we may not see each other again.

—Goodbye grandma – he approaches and hugs her; she withdraws abruptly and wipes away her tears.

—Goodbye, Mama Joaquina – the Black woman kisses his forehead and tells him:

—May God be with you mijo.

Chapter 15

The Shipwreck

The group of young people has spent months in Spain improving their knowledge of the language and with their friends they have prepared the long-awaited trip and they have spent a couple of weeks in the port called Palos de Moguer or "de la Frontera" from where the boats led by Cristóbal Columbus left on Friday, August 3, 1492. They have enrolled in a commemorative trip to the event, which intends to make the admiral's journey on the same date, but in 1889. They, along with other young people from all over Europe, will repeat the 27 days forgotten that the first three ships passed in Africa before leaving the Mediterranean, so the final departure for America will be on September 6, 1889. They would also pass through the Canary Islands and make a brief stay, a fact that they forget when they relate the trips to the first ships that crossed the Atlantic Ocean.

The young people gather in the Church of San Jorge Mártir to pray and commend themselves to God before the trip. Jean had not used to asking for anything, but this time he kneels and prays for his new destiny, because like the first sailors he knows that he will cross the Atlantic for the first time and in his heart, he fears that the course of him can be lose.

The group is excited about the trip, and they have planned how they are going to document the journey, as well as how they are going to manage food and water, since each one oversees their survival on the high seas. The first route out of Spain to Africa is short and picturesque. The biggest challenge is to avoid storms in the open ocean, for which they are been training in the days leading up to the final game. Jean is a detailed young man and has decided to write his own diary and collect all his experiences.

Wednesday, September 6, 1889.

Finally, we left Africa. The last point we arrived at is the Isla de las Palomas, where we made a short stop and at sunset we left for the vast Atlantic. The night is starry, and winter is already beginning, so it is getting cold quickly. We traveled on the Dutch sailboat Tres Amigos, wide sails, tall masts, and long wooden hulls. It is of amazing design, and one of the most exotic in Europe today.

...

Tuesday, September 19, 1889.

"Three days ago, it has been raining nonstop and we have informed that a storm is coming. I must confess that it is frightening, especially at night because the stars are not visible, and the darkness does not allow us to see beyond our noses. Everything is wet, we have been wearing the same clothes for days and we have not been able to dry them, so it must be that we are more tired because of the weight we have on us."

That Tuesday night the ship was engulfing by a great storm and without being able to avoid it, the young people were floating adrift on the high seas, among them the young Jean. They have lost count of the hours they have been on top of a piece of wood receiving the sun's rays and the rain. They begin to lose consciousness at times and hallucinate.

...

A week later Jean is on another sailboat heading to his destination, but he has lost all his belongings. The hours without eating, the sun and serene has created a mental block. They knew his name because his shirt bears the dedication of his grandmother. The young man dehydrated and has been sleeping for days.

On November 10, 1889, they arrived at a port in the east of the island where the sailboat was heading with hired laborers to work in the cane fields. Jean's Spanish is not perfect, but he can have a good relationship with the contractors and gets a job on the crew. He really does not remember much of who he is, nor the reason he undertook the journey. Thus, he has begun his new life, as an immigrant who has arrived with nothing.

Chapter 16

The Creole Loves

December 2, 1892

Two years have passed since Jean arrived on the island, in his work as an assistant in the sugar mill he has progressed, he was promoting to centrifuge operator, because in a brief time he has understood the process and understands the operation of the machinery at the perfection. Jean does not remember his past, and it does not seem to interest him because he has inserted himself very well into the society of the village where he lives, there he has a good friend, Mr. Evaristo, who hired him and brought him to live in his house in what got a permanent place.

The foreman, as everyone calls him, is a mestizo man, corpulent and with large mustaches, he is married to a Spanish woman and has two daughters, the eldest is called Isabel, she is a beautiful young woman who from the first day fixed her eyes on the forgetful that her Father brought French to the house, as his friends call him, because sometimes he responds with words in that language, especially when he is upset. Jean regularly visits the friend's house and looks for reasons to be close to the young woman who no longer knows what to do to get her attention.

It is Sunday and as usual the people walk around the park. "Today I'll talk to her" Jean thinks as he walks to meet the young woman:

—Miss, can I walk next to you?

—Gladly sir.

—The afternoon is very cool and beautiful ladies like you stand out in the light of the setting sun.

—Thank you, you are very eloquent.

So, in the cadence of slow steps, between praise and warm looks, the young people began a romance that would take them to the altar and keep a family together until old age.

When the Frenchman was 70 years old, one afternoon he called his grandson, Jean (the young architect father), and confessed that he had remembered who he was and that his family owned a coffee plantation in the east of the country, but that he did not remember the name of the place. The father kept the secret.

Chapter 17

The Mystery of The Tombs

Los Naranjos, October 6, 1987

Ernesto holds one end of the ribbon and Jean, the other end of the façade, takes the length of the canvas. The teacher draws the sketch and notes the measurements. It is two in the afternoon on the third day. The teacher has her hair tied up inside a "Yarey" hat (a straw hat). Jean places his hand to cover the Sun while he measures, and she holds out the hat to him.

—Thank you – says the young man.

The woman's black hair moves in the wind and her flushed cheeks highlight her black eyes. The young man stands for a moment looking at the teacher's silhouette against the light and he is going to lose his balance.

—Let us go in, the sun is hurting you.

—"Wait" – he tries to pull out a small blade tangled in her hair. The teacher looks at him and smiles.

He is standing with the sun at his back and his blond hair shines like gold. The woman looks down and enters the house.

The cold and dark atmosphere of the room attracts and envelopes them, the nearby bodies absorbed with an immense desire to touch. She walks over and almost touches his back. Clara and Andrés enter, and her steps stop the raised hand that trembles with the proximity of the desired body.

– "We found two tombs behind the quartiers."

—The black knows who they are.

—He only talks about the Frenchman lost in the coffee plantation.

He says that when the full moon rises, the Frenchman wanders through the coffee plantation.

—Slave stories... let us see the tombs.

They hurried past the garden, through the quartiers and into a small forest where wild plants and fungi cover two blackened tombstones on the reddish earth. The young people clean the surface and remain silent when reading what the first tombstone says: "To my beloved Carmen, light of my mornings, sun of my evening." Quickly they cleaned the other one and read: "Jean Joubert." Jean turns slowly and sees the pallor and astonishment reflected on the face of Carmen, the teacher. The others rush to clean the glass that covers the photos of Jean and his wife. They are amazed at the resemblance to the professor and the young architecture student. Nobody says a word. Carmen falls to the ground and ask them to leave her alone.

...

It has gotten dark, and Jean is leaning on the iron balustrade on the second level of the mansion. His mind works quickly. The name of Jean Joubert is an inherited from his great-grandfather who arrived on the island at the end of the 19th century and settled in the capital of the province, where the family has always lived. No one ever mentioned coffee plantations, nor the existence of a relative who had lived on the island before.

Carmen, without losing her calm, sits on the stairs, thinking about the scientific possibilities for the coincidence of the names, and more than that, the coincidence of the age difference. The other members of the group have gone to the barracks to gossip and try to discover the intrigue that surrounds them, there is no lack of laughter and dark jokes. The night, an accomplice of history, is cloudy and thunder continuously sounds that illuminate the valley and reveal the coming rain.

Whatever the story, they are willing to discover it. The peasants announced to the group that it will rain for days, and they will not be able to leave the valley. They agree to rest for the night, without talking about it, and the next day plan to investigate further. Everyone goes to sleep and in the silence of the mansion the spell of a story that no one has told perceived. Jean falls asleep staring at the place where Carmen is, although he cannot see her. She just closes her eyes and remembers wanting to touch Jean's back.

Chapter 18

The Rider and The Storm

Los Naranjos, October 7, 1987

The rain falls intensely, rays and lightning frighten the group that investigates Los Naranjos. Instinctively everyone has gathered in a corner of what used to be the warehouse on the first level of the mansion, focused on the door that lets them see the flashes of light and where the strong wind of the storm enters. The young Marianela from the farmhouse distracted talking and was stuck with them.

Rains in the coffee plantations are common, but when storms with almost hurricane-force winds break out, feared. Young people not accustomed to country life are terrified because the poor visibility and the continuous noise of lightning represent an unknown scene for them. Refugees in their corner try to give themselves courage. For a moment, the aftermath of lightning allows them to see the rider standing in the middle of the storm, defying nature.

—Hey look at that. — Clara says — it looks like a man on a horse.

—"Yes,"— the rest agree as they look at the door, and again, the light from the lightning lets them see the rider standing in the middle of the gale.

He is a naked man on horseback — says Ernesto — it is just that everything is very dark.

—He is a naked man on horseback — explains Marianela.

—He is crazy, who would think of going out in the middle of this storm and with this rain to ride — comments Carmen.

—You have said it, he is crazy — affirms Marianela — nobody knows where he comes from, he only appears when there are storms and walks naked through the coffee plantation. No one has really seen him up close.

As fate would have it, lightning strikes the rider and he falls to the ground during the noise, the young people in disbelief of what they have just seen, get up and run to the gate. The storm is getting more intense but deciding that it is necessary to help the fallen rider, the men grab a blanket and go out in search of the fallen body. The horse is dead, but the naked man is alive.

The women prepare a bed where they accommodate the man, making sure that he is well covered, and they begin to rub him with the same clothes with which they have covered him. Marianela stares at him and in amazement she says:

—He looks like Jean.

—It is your idea, look, he is a "mulato" and has very curly black hair — says Clara.

—It does look alike, if you look closely, they have the same nose and mouth — continues explaining —Marianela — it is the first time I have seen it, the only one who has seen it before is old Ramon because he leaves him clothes and food I do not know where in the mountain.

—I do not see the resemblance — Clara insists.

Carmen comes over with hot tea in a pot and tries to give him a drink. She then sits next to the young men and continue to stare at the fallen one and comments:

—This man is at least 60 years old, and if for a mestizo, his lips are very thin, and his nose is Greek like Jean's.

—Who will this man be? — Ernesto says — he is extraordinarily strong, and although he looks older, his muscles are strong.

—He should do exercise, at least he should walk.

—What happens is that the peasants here go up and down hills – explains Marianela – that keeps them strong and even if they are old, they can still pick the coffee and do other tasks.

The man begins to cough and Carmen approaches with more tea. He sits and looks at them in amazement:

—Who are you? What are they doing in the house? Only Ramon and I come here, no one else passes by.

She moves with the intention of standing up but remembers that he is naked. As she moves, she looks up and meets this young man who seems to have come out of the painting that her mother kept of the former owner of the coffee plantation, young Jean, and she also calls him "Mesié." Accustomed by now to the resemblance, the young people are not surprised this time, but instead begin to question the "mulato."

—And who are you? Why didn't anyone tell us that you would walk through the coffee plantations without clothes?

—No one comes here, only Ramon and this daring woman, who knows not to go where no one call her.

—Why am I not coming? Look at the storm that is falling, be thankful that we were here. Who was going to help you? You would have died.

—It is not the first time I have struck by lightning, the poor beast always saves me, this time it seems like he could not take it anymore.

—Well, what is your name? Jean asks.

—Juan, like my father and my grandfather. These lands belonged to my great-grandfather Jean Joubert, he died in the coffee plantation fire, and then the madam took the child, but my great-grandfather, my grandfather and my father took care of this place, and now it is my turn.

—How, you are a descendant of the owner?

—Young Jean had a black woman who comforted him before his wife arrived, what happened was that with the tragedy everything was forgotten and no one remembered the black woman anymore, she went to the mountains for fear that they would take the baby away from her, and no one ever heard from her again, but there with other blacks they set up a *palenque*, up on the mountain. Later, over the years, the others left, but my father insisted that someone would recover the coffee plantation and here I have waited all this time.

Chapter 19

Attracted by The Name

Los Naranjos, October 8, 1987

The rooster is not crowing this morning, it is still raining, and the faint sun barely enters through the cracks in the wood of the mansion. Jean does not stop looking at the corner where Carmen is. She knows that the young man is watching her and is afraid of turning her body to the side where he is. The rest pretend to sleep, no one wants to be the first to wake up and draw the attention of others. The sound of the big door opening gives everyone a chance to feign surprise and get up. The Black man has come in with his granddaughter and they have brought hot coffee in metal mugs.

Sitting in a circle, they drink coffee and eat cornbread that the young woman distributes with a smile. Black at last says:

–My grandfather told the story of the Frenchman who went crazy and set fire to the coffee plantation, burning himself with it. They never found his body. But he was crazy, he lay on his wife's grave and sang in French day and night. It is not known where they took the son, they never returned. The administrator was on the farm until they began to burn the coffee plantations with the war of independence, and the Spanish looted everything they could before leaving the area. The mansion was close and forgotten for about a century, they say that it is haunted and that the spirit of the French does not allow anyone to inhabit it.

No more they said, no one asks, no one comments, they take their coffee and bread and go out in silence, only Carmen and Jean remain.

—How is it possible that without having worked before and without specialty being in a construction of French coffee plantations, you have become interested in this project?

—The name of the coffee plantation attracted me, I wanted to know why it is call Los Naranjos.

—The name? It seems pointless to me, getting involved in an investigation into something that no one seems to be interested in just because of a name.

—Yes, the name echoed in my head as if to tell me, there is something there that interests me.

—But you did not know that the owner was name like you?

—It was part of what we need to investigate, it is the only settlement for which there is no property registry, and nobody wants to come to it because of its intricacy. In addition, they are only ruins, nothing salvageable had preserved.

Jean, then why risk the investigation if there are other places with better conditions.

—I do not know, from the beginning I forgot the names of all the others, and I insisted on looking for and getting to Los Naranjos.

—We must be aim, discover the chance factor that surrounds us.

—Carmen, excuse me for calling you by your name, but you do not think that there is something else that unites us, something beyond the call of the name.

—Jean do not forget the most important thing is the work we came to do. What this place can contribute to the investigation. Let us not be the object of the game of destiny.

Jean walks over and stares at her: Why isn't she married? She answers as she was knowing his thinking:

—I do not believe in love. I just love my career and the things that I can achieve with my effort. If I were married, I could not be here. Love is a difficult bond to dissolve.

—I imagined it, a woman without dreams, which is why she never smiles.

—My smile is the trophy for those I let into my life, and my students are not part of them.

—Will there be someone who can unleash that smile?

—Not in this place.

—We do not know.

It is the fourth day, and the water runs from the mountains to the plain where the house is. The peasants run in search of the students and the teacher announcing that a great flood is coming, and they must go out with them. The adventure is over, they can do nothing but return to the city. They leave with the firm intention of returning and discovering the mystery that the coffee plantation keeps.

Chapter 20

Jean discovers the secret of his father

What happened in Los Naranjos was a surprise for the young architecture student and when he got home, he told his father in detail about the experience, noticing a strange expression on his face that did not disappear with the passing of days, so he decided to investigate the reason for that expression of concern.

—Dad, I have noticed you upset for days, I see you looking in the drawers and we hardly talk. Is something wrong that you have not told me?

—Your great-grandfather, the Frenchman, before dying told me one day that he had remembered the reason why he had embarked here, he told me that his family had some coffee plantations in the east of the country, but that he did not know where, I did not even remember the name, so I did not give it importance, but now that you tell me about the coincidence of the names and the other things, I wonder if it had something to do with what he told me.

—But dad, how have you kept quiet about something like that for so many years? Imagine if that is not the farm he came looking for.

—Well, coincidences exist, the most difficult thing is that we have no way of knowing if that is the place, the truth is that I was never interested in knowing anything about its history before arriving in the country because since he did not remember it, in addition many people who immigrated from Europe to here, they had nothing in their countries and they came to make a new life here, I thought that possibly he did not want to remember something that might be painful or shameful from his past.

—In any case, we must investigate, who knows and really, I have a relationship with the tormented Frenchman from Los Naranjos.

—Son, you have a way of saying things. But if it is time to seek help on this matter, I have been looking for old documents, but I remember that they always told me that he shipwrecked and all the documents that he had with him were lose, that the name was known from an embroidered shirt that he was wearing.

—The best thing would be to write to the French embassy and seek advice.

Thus began the investigations that ended up discovering that indeed, the young student was a descendant of the family that owned the coffee plantation, although he could only know it through the testimonies of the peasants of the place since there was no record of anything related to the place. They were also able to contact French relatives who at once rushed to do their own research to meet the descendants of the young man who set out one day in search of his forgotten heritage.

Chapter 21

An Unexpected Visit

Jean and his father have been preparing their trip to Paris for days. They are full of emotion to meet the family they did not know they had in the old continent, because not only in France but also in Spain they have found relatives. It is early and they must do last-minute paperwork, but someone unexpectedly arrives at their door, a lady in her fifties, very well dressed and accompanied by an obviously foreign man. Jean's father collapses on the sofa in the small living room, speechless with astonishment. The young man lets the couple pass and asks who they are.

—I am your mother...

—The silence is the protagonist of the moment and the young man only answers:

—Come on, who will explain to me what all this means. Dad, did you know about this?

—No, he does not know anything, look at him, don't you realize that he is in shock?

—I imagine that you will have an explanation for showing up like that out of nowhere in this house.

—Of course, I have an explanation. For years I wanted to contact you, but it has been difficult for me, until thank God, I have had the resources to come.

—What do you think she is going to tell us now? Let us see, tell me, ma'am, how could you forget a son for almost twenty years?

—But I never forgot you, you have been present in my mind every moment since I left this house.

Well, let us sit down and talk quietly — Jean the father finally says — Blanca, what is that prevented you from communicating for so long? I never imagined that you would forget your son like this, I always knew that our marriage would not last, we were quite different, and I knew that you were looking for something beyond what I could offer you.

—Jean, the time we lived together you know that I did my best because we were a happy family, but when I had the opportunity to go to Spain I did not think twice, but always with the idea that you would join me later.

—So when you changed your mind and forgot about the family you left here?

—If you let me explain you will understand the reasons.

—Well, speak for once...

—When I arrived in Spain, I only knew about my father's family with whom I had contacted, they lived in the Canary Islands, in Tenerife, and I arrived there. They received me like a distant relative and days later they told me that I had to work to be able to live there and pay them what they had lent me for the papers and the trip. I did not know anything, and I went to the street to see what was appearing, passing by a bar I saw an announcement that they were looking for waitresses and I went in, I talked to the manager, and he told me that I could do the job, but that I had to start at dawn because It was what they had available at the moment. That is how it was, then I had already settled in a room with another young woman, and I thought that I would be on my way to be able to make money, pay the debt and see how I could get together to send for you.

—And what happened, why didn't you send for us?

—I met a girl from Morocco who told me that there was another way to make quick money, and she convinced me to travel with her to a city called Casablanca, that there was an acquaintance of hers who was proposing a business to her. I took the little saved I had and went with her. I was excited because I had seen a movie with that name, and I thought it was a good sign.

—Casablanca. The place of the film?

—That same onc, is a genuinely lovely place but dangerous. When we arrived, they took away our passports saying that they would give it to us when we went back, then they dressed us as Arabs and told us not to talk so they would not realize we were from Spain. Already at that moment it began to scare me a little, but my friend told me not to worry that she had already gone there for the merchandise times. However, as we entered the streets, I felt worse and I started to say that I wanted to leave, but they had my money and my documents, there was nothing I could do. Then they took me to a place that I never knew where it was and they locked us in a room, I do not know for how long. Then they put us in the truck and took us to another part where I finally realized that it would not be easy for me to get out of there, they took us to a brothel.

Chapter 22

The Years in Morocco

Blanca and her friend María Elena have been deceived and taken to prostitution in Casablanca, they do not speak Arabic and have gone through a lot of work to get along with the rest of the women in the brothel, they are still young, and the men are looking for them, but the atmosphere between the women other women is not good and they have not been welcomed. To survive, they have stuck together, giving each other strength, and sometimes nursing the wounds caused by clients when they refuse to satisfy their vilest desires.

The two women have stayed in the back room of the house, the smallest, in which there is a personal bed and many other things in boxes that they have not wanted to investigate, they only go there to rest the little time they have, because no matter the time of day, if someone requests them, they must go. This situation has made the two women take care of each other and live together as true sisters. The Spaniard is older than the islander and she knows more about the ways of the Arabs, and she always says that one day someone will come who will get her out of that pigsty.

But twelve years have passed, and they are still in the same situation, with the difference that they are no longer so young, and the clients have less money and are from a lower class. María Elena is extremely sick, and she can hardly leave the room, she lives off the little food that her friend can bring her, and she does not even have the strength to get out of bed.

—Look Blanca, in this suitcase are the most important things in my life, there is a piece of paper on which I have written the address of my family in Madrid, I don't know if they are still there, but if you manage to get out of here one day, take them this letter, there I explain everything, and I know they will help you.

—But woman, how havc you saved so much money?

—You know, I only bought the essentials and the Moor who liked me always left me something in my bed, you know that forbidden them to pay us, but he always gave me something hidden.

—Do not worry, we are going to get out of here together, with this money I will see how I manage and get out of this.

—No, I am going to die in this room, you do not let them discover the money or the letter I gave you, your freedom depends on that.

—But woman, if you have endured all this time, you are not going to give up the desire to get out of here, look at everything you have gathered.

—I wish I had decided before, wait a long time and look now — sighs — "I'm dying"

María Elena knew that she would not take it anymore and the last two days she instructed Blanca so that she could escape. "El moro," as they called the old man who was looking for her, already had instructions that, if she died, he should look for her contacts to help "La isleña" as they knew the other woman in the place. Years had passed since they had been slaves to that place, and they were older and worn out, they hardly paid attention to them, they had them as servants cleaning the place and cooking or washing clothes.

When the Spanish woman died, Blanca contacted the Moro and they began to make arrangements for their escape, but it was not easy because they never left the area around the house and, if she did manage to leave, she does not have documents to travel, so she will have to go out on the traffickers' boats and when they arrive in Spain find a way to get some documentation, which will not be easy, since many years have passed since they made the first Spanish document and passport.

The islander has lost her friend and she know that if she does not do anything to get out of that place now that she has a chance, she never will. She decided to give part of the money to the Moro and prays that, for the memory of the Spaniard, he helps her. But a month passes, and the man does not appear with news and begins to get impatient, he does not know what to do, everyday life becomes less bearable in that infernal place, he feels alone.

—Little Madonna Maria — she prays — do not abandon me, look that I have always carried you in my thoughts and I know that you have taken care of my life in this place of the devil. I only ask you one thing, take me to the island to see my son, only that, if I must die later, I will die in peace. — Night after night is Blanca's prayer, she is alone in the small room, she prays and prays the same.

Tonight, as usual they have come to take out the closed boxes and leave empty boxes in the room, every two weeks the same for 15 years. She remembers what María Elena said: "Surely what they have there is drugs, but how do we know, if we open them, they will realize, you know that the Moors who come are prohibited from opening the boxes, they only take them to the boat... and look, we fit perfectly there, one day we should get in and be taken..."

The islander stared at the empty boxes and climbed into one of them to make sure there really was room for her to snuggle in there. The most awkward thing she thought was: "How do I close the box afterwards?" Still, she has two weeks to find a solution.

As the days went by, she made plans first, to hide one of the boxes, lest they not take it away empty. To keep the address, the letter, and the money in such a way that, if they discovered it, it would not lose. The best thing she could think of was to wrap it in nylon and insert it into her vagina, not in the anus, because: "What is It goes in, and I have to fart?" It was still heavy on my mind... "How the hell do I close the box?"

In the afternoon, a little boy always comes to take away the garbage, he hardly speaks, but he has become friends with Blanca because she gives him candy and lets him watch the circus cartoons on the small portable television he has in his room. She has been evaluating the boy, about 10 years old to see if she can close the box for him and she gives him the little television.

—It is just that I want to scare the Moor, you know, I want to go out when they come to pick up the boxes.

—Hahahaha, that would be brutal, because that Moor is a coward... but would you really give me the TV?

—Yes son, yes. I am thinking of buying another one. Do not worry, just nail the lid of the box well.

—Well, when do you want to scare him?

—On Friday when they come for the full boxes, I am going to hide an empty one and when they bring the full ones, I go in and you cover the box for me, so they take me with them.

—Ok, but what if they find out?

—You do not worry I tell them that you were helping me with the joke.

When the day came when they would come to pick up the full boxes, Blanca waited for the Moors to bring the boxes full of drugs and took out the one she had hidden a few days ago, the garbage boy came and as soon as it got dark, she settled down and the hill the box by hammering hard on the nails she had prepared, then grabbed her TV and left. A couple of hours later the Moors arrived and took the boxes away. For the islander, everything was a move and pull until they reached the boat, there she was lucky that they put her box under the others, so the weight helped so that it would not move so much, but so that it would not open.

Drug traffickers transport hashish from Mar Chica, in Morocco, to the Spanish coast and normally do so in boats equipped with five motors that reach speeds of sixty knots (almost 120 kilometers per hour), so they moved to Ibiza, the Valencian coast, from there to the Ebro Delta in Catalonia, where they unloaded the merchandise. They left her in a hidden place near the river in a natural park, where a van came to pick her up and take her to Madrid, about 6 more hours and finally they began to uncover the wooden boxes one by one until they met the islander.

Chapter 23

The Islander in Madrid

Blanca has been left with very little money, she has had to pay the value of thirty thousand dollars for the lost cargo in the box in which she left Casablanca and ten thousand dollars to have her Spanish passport remade with her identity, not you will be able to survive more than a few days with the little money you have left. She decided to go in search of María Elena's family with the address she wrote on the small piece of paper.

The address is in the Salamanca neighborhood, in the middle of the city, so she decides to leave Latina early and look for a taxi to take her there. She doesn't know what to expect after almost 16 years since her friend spoke for the last time with her mother and brother, she doesn't know if they are still in that direction, but she thinks that now María Elena is like an angel who will guide her to fulfill what she promised her friend on her deathbed.

Finally, she is in front of the house, when she touches her a man a little older than her comes out but who at once reminds her of the smile of her great friend:

—You must be Paco because you are the male version of María Elena.

—Yes, yes ma'am, I am myself, and do you know about my sister?

—Yes, a brief time ago we shared a room, but unfortunately, I am here today because she did not get to see this day.

—What happened? We have not heard from her for years, mom died wanting to see her again and I stayed here just because it was her and me, you found me by chance because yesterday I had to leave for Valencia, I work at the port. But woman, what sad news have you brought me? How is it that María E has not communicated with us in so long?

—It is something I must tell you calmly, it has not been easy, she really was my best friend and thanks to her I am here, I owe her.

But sit down, you must tell me everything in detail, I am incredibly sad to know that my María E, as I called her, is dead, although I thought that she had died a long time ago because I have not been able to understand how she did not communicate with me again. her mother if she called her every day. We even went to look for her where she lived in Tenerife, but they told us that she had gone to work outside the country, only nobody knew where.

—Yes, we ended up in Casablanca in Morocco, but they really tricked us, and we were slaves to those Moors for years.

—What a horrible woman, and how my poor little sister could bear that, she was very fragile.

—That is precisely why I cannot stand it, she gave me money for you, but misfortune did not allow me to bring it, but I promise you that as soon as I can, I will find it for you.

—Woman do not worry. If I see that you are really in need, I do not need that money. Knowing that you were with her when she had no family near her, for me, is worth more than money.

—Paco, you are a good man, and I do not want you to think that I take advantage of her good heart, because what she did for me is the greatest thing that anyone has been able to give me in my entire life.

After this first visit, Blanca visited Paco sometimes because he wanted to know increasingly about what her sister's life had been like during those years that she was away from him and her mother. One day Paco invited her to stay, and they realized that they wanted to be more than friends, so the island woman once again felt the desire to love a man and have sex with him without the remorse or pain she felt when she was mistreated by those rough, smelly men using her for their evil pleasure in Casablanca.

Chapter 24

Blanca and Paco

The islander has gone to live in Paco's house, he spends the whole week working at the port and comes on weekends, so she also works as a server in a hotel and has been able to raise money to travel to the island in search of his son. He only torments her that he has not yet told the Spaniard her desire to travel and every day he sees that the relationship between them is becoming more intense and dependent, the man thinks that he has found a partner for the rest of his life.

That afternoon he arrived with a bouquet of flowers and a bottle of wine. He says that he has something important that he wants to celebrate. Wanting to please him, she has prepared a potato omelet with the Creole touch as she calls it and has dressed very provocatively to please him. She knows that when she lets her hair down and puts on the miniskirts, he loses his sanity and cannot stand the urge to take her to bed. his time, he sat down. while having a glass of wine, he takes a little red box out of his pocket and kneeling he asks her:

—Blanca, will you marry me?

She, stunned, has dropped into the chair, and taking her hands has made him stand up while she tells him:

—My dear Paco, you know that I love you with all my soul, but there is something I have not told you and it is time you knew it.

—What woman? What is it that you have not told me? Do you have another man?

—In a way, yes, I am still married in my country, and I also have a son there.

—But woman, why haven't you told me that? Why let me fall in love with you?

—I know I should have told you, but I let myself enveloped by this feeling that you provoked in me and every day I say to myself: “Today I am going to tell him.” And since you arrived, I have not been able to.

—You see, now that I have decided for the first time in my life to start a family, I cannot, you already have a family.

—It is complicated, I have not had communication with them for many years, I am even afraid to contact them, I have thought to raise the money and go there and explain everything to see if they forgive me and understand me, but my dear Paco, do not worry, that man must have found another woman and may even have more family.

—You mean that if you divorce, we can we get married?

—Of course, my love, I could not live apart from you anymore.

—Well, say no more, we are going to the island to resolve your divorce and so you can see your son.

Chapter 25

The Farewell

The University, Summer 1988

The graduates leave the theater hugging and kissing. In each mouth the word "Congratulations". At the exit door, Jean waits for Carmen who approaches him dressed in red with her hair down covering her bare back. Her tight dress draws her figure, and the young man enjoys her rhythmic walk. "Nobody would say that he is thirty years old "—he thinks. When she arrives, she leans over to pick up her bag on the table, and he takes the opportunity to approach her from behind, she turns quickly, and her eyes meet once again.

—Professor Carmen.

—Hello student... excuse me architect – She hangs her bag from her shoulder and prepares to walk. Jean blocks her path.

—Today, I go.

—Thanks to God.

—I did not know you believed in God

—There are better not to announce what we believe and just live it.

—My father says the same.

—And you? Do you believe in something?

—In love. Is it time for us to talk?

—No, I do not know, I do not know yet.

—Anyway, this week my father and I left for France. We finally found information about my great-grandfather's family. The poor man had lost his memory, but with what happened in Los

Naranjos everything began to become known, and we contacted our relatives in Paris.

—I am glad, I hope you can find your roots, at least that is what the trip to the coffee plantation served us for.

—Is there any way we can have contact?

No, for now, focus on your family and the projects you have ahead of you, maybe when you return, if the opportunity arises, we will talk.

—But...

—No, let time show us what is best. For now, it is goodbye.

She walks away from him, and he follows her with his eyes until she is losing in the crowd of families celebrating their recent graduates, then he sees his father that he finds no one to talk to and goes towards:

—Dad, you seem lost in the middle of these people, come let us say hello to Odalis and Clara who are taking photos.

Saying this to the father, they stop to see Blanca who arrives with Paco. Jean did not know he was coming because he had not invited them.

—Dad, who told the lady to come? How did she find out about the graduation?

—I invited her; she is interested in approaching you. She says that she does not know how to make up for the time she wasted with you.

Jean sees them arrive and although he did not expect their assistance, he is happy to be able to have both, father, and mother with him that day, something that he had never imagined, at that moment he thought of all that they had talked about and the things that the woman told him. she had told how difficult it had been for her to meet him again. He thanked life for this new opportunity and reaching out to his mother, he hugged her.

Chapter 26

Jeans in Paris. The surprise of Fate

Jean and his father have arrived in Paris, he is greeting at the airport by Evonne and Fabienne, the only relatives he was able to contact after digging. They, knowing of the existence of the islanders, also sought the evidence to prove that they were the descendants of the intrepid young man who left the country a century ago and never heard from again. Everyone believed him dead, but the story that the old would repeat and would remember for more than a century always remained.

The house where Madame Joubert lived before her grandson left for the island was still inhabited by other relatives, because when she died, her nephews inherited the property and lived in it, a place where they welcomed the new relatives with open arms and eager to know the story of the one, they thought had died on the journey, or God knows otherwise, because they never heard from him again.

Arriving at the location, young Jean was amazed at how well preserved the apartment was, which in the late 19th century considered a luxury on Rue Laffitte. Upon entering the apartment, time had stopped, the family had decided to keep the place as Madame Joubert had left it a hundred years ago, with adjustments, because no one had really inhabited it permanently. Upon entering, a portrait of the lady and what was surely the dead young man in the coffee plantation caught our attention, which really did look like a photo of the young architect who impressed.

The apartment dazzles the young man because it is a true example of Art Nouveau architecture in Paris, known by nature, flowers, trees and other plant references that usually expressed sinuous and dynamic motifs and patterns that looked to get rid of rigor that dominated earlier styles. The relatives notice the boy's interest and praise him for knowing him, something that pleases his father, but annoys Jean.

Like the buildings of the period, this one is asymmetrical, with balconies on the facades and the entrance found on a corner. Decorated with bars, walkways and window frames in different shapes and made of cast iron with curved lines. The apartment occupies the fourth and final floor, part of which is the back garden, where they go out and sit around a round table where cheese and ham served. Other members of the family have gathered and all question the newcomers, excited to learn the story of the lost young man who set out in search of his estate and lost his memory and all connection to his family.

After hours, family begin to leave and Fabienne informs them that they will be able to stay in the apartment for as long as they consider necessary to take steps to recover the identity of Jean's great-grandfather and find out what they could recover from the heritage on the island or in France. The newcomers are relieved to be alone and free from questions, they sit finishing the bottle of wine and looking at the lights of the city. None of them want to talk, they really are so surprised by everything that has happened to them in the last week that they just want peace to think about what they should do.

—It is my idea dad, but these people have received us with great enthusiasm.

—It may be that way here, but, looking at it well, if a little more than usual... it may be.

—Anyway, we must be alert to anything, lest we get a surprise.

That night Jean delighted in observing the lights of Paris and the details of the apartment that had belonged to his family and that he and his father now lived in, something that he had not imagined before and that, by fate and his interest in constructions French coffee plantations and especially Los Naranjos, now you can enjoy.

The next morning Evonne and Fabienne pick them up to take them to the civil registry offices and other places to show the relationship and find out their status in terms of obtaining French citizenship. To their astonishment it would not be exceedingly difficult. They recommended to seek a lawyer, in Madame Joubert's will, there was a clause in case her son appeared, or any descendant of his, clause of which the French knew the existence of, but did not know the real content.

—Then it means that you knew that if an heir of the lady appeared, that clause of the will had to open.

—We know that it exists because for a long time members of the family have tried to find out where part of the fortune that could not be found is, but the law office that still keeps the will and has it registered in the General Registry of Acts of Last Will, where only the notary of the office in charge with the willed heir can give in, as I understand it, Madame Joubert left a document explaining that up to the fourth generation of her son's descendants could access that part of the estate.

—Does that mean that my dad and I are still heirs to the fortune of the owners of Los Naranjos?

Yes, and believe me, the relatives are interested in knowing if you really are descendants of the lady's son.

—I already imagined that so much honey last night was for something...

—Yes, my sister and I have had resistance since we began to have contact with you, but we did not want to tell you anything so that you could make the trip in peace, and we could find the papers in peace.

—Anyway, thank you for telling us so we will know what to expect with others.

Later, in the notary's office, the document read where the late Madame Joubert set up that if at any time a survivor appeared. The coffee plantation "Los Naranjos", and the apartment in Paris will give to that person, like the summer house in Saint-Tropez, which had been use by the family, but still could not pass ownership because the generations mentioned by the will had not yet passed. The heaviest procedure was still looking for more evidence to show that Jean and his father were descendants of the landowner who owned the coffee plantation and son of the deceased.

A couple of weeks would pass, and father and son were still in negotiations, which would lengthen their trip, so they decided to get to know the city, and the other members of the family, who, either out of interest or out of solidarity, always shook their hands and They helped where they could. Jean, the young man, began to learn French and managed to contact "Arquitectura sin Fronteras" an organization that was beginning to take shape by a group of architects who worked for sustainable development collaborating with other Spanish associations in Andalusia, with the desire to become present in different countries through cooperation projects, to work with thousands of people a year in search of improving their living conditions and other fundamental rights.

The fundamental objective of the organization would be to defend the right to decent housing and to the city; and to cooperate in the field of social architecture, with housing projects, schools, health centers, sanitation networks or education and training; ideas that caught the young man from his time as a student and that he longs to be able to put into projects that revive the cities of his island and above all that revive the settlements in the countryside.

Jean had begun to have contact with a Colombian architect residing in Paris and upon his arrival he did not take long to look for her, she in turn introduced him to the rest of the team and they began to look for common interests in the realization of projects, which in his measure also allowed Jean to consider the idea of using what was left of Los Naranjos as an incentive for the creation of some tourist project or something in the place, if he managed to get the rights to the property, which not only depended on proved he was a descendant of the former owner, but also of the laws of the island in relation to foreign property.

Chapter 27

Jean (father) and the French

The old man, as Jean calls his father, walks through the "Champs De Mars" or "Champs de Mars", one of his favorite places in Paris, he can see many people running, reading, or simply walking their children, like the young lady who walks a child in a wheelchair, several times they have crossed paths and she has greeted him. He has not dared to speak to her because his French is not very good, but this afternoon she has stayed longer near the bench where he is and has been able to look at her more carefully, she is very tall and seems to be between 35 and 40 years old, short black hair, the boy has the same hair color and looks like her, maybe 12 years old. The woman approches :

—Salut monsieur, pouvez-vous me regarder l'enfant un instant, s'il vous plait...

—Désolé, je ne parle pas français ...

—Spanish? Speak Spanish?

—Yes

—That, if you can look at the child for a moment, I forgot the bag on the other bench, there.

Yes go

The woman takes quick steps and comes back with the heavy bag.

—It is that I bring him his food, he hardly eats and when we come here, he entertains himself and eats better.

—His Spanish is particularly good

It is that I lived in Spain for a long time, he was born there.

—I was born on a Caribbean Island, and this is the first time I have come to Paris.

—And do you like it?

—Yes, I had read about the city, but the truth is that it seemed much better than what I had read and seen in the movies.

—I was born here in Paris, but my parents took me to Spain when I was very young and there I got married and had Jesus, he is my only son and he has paralysis in his legs because he fell off the balcony of some neighbors while playing and I am left in that condition, They have done many tests, but there is no hope, he has mobility from the waist up, and he likes being outside a lot. He also speaks Spanish.

—Hello Jesus, my name is Jean.

—Hi sir...

—It is good that you like to come to the park, so you are surround by happy people and nature. —There is space, and the air is fresh.

—I like to steep my Cerf Volant...

—Oh, the kite...

—It is that he likes to see how the wind carries him, but sometimes he has gone, and we have lost him.

—Come, I will help you, I like it too, when I was a child, my father always made me paper ones.

—Jesus, what is your mother's name?

—Her name is Camille.

Jean plays with the child for a while. The mother a tablecloth on the lawn and arranges the food. She has bread, cheese, and Quiche Lorraine, which Jesus likes very much. She served three dishes and juices from the basket.

—Mr. Jean, will you join us?

—Yes, of course that looks delicious. What is it? Like a Spanish omelet?

—The Quiche Lorraine? No, it seems, but is short crust pastry filled with fresh cream, eggs and bacon seasoned with black pepper and nutmeg. Try it.

Jean takes a picce of the cake that Camille has put on a small plate for him.

—The truth is as good as it seems, I liked it.

—I like it, it is what I like the most.

—I see Jesus and what else do you like to eat?

—Ice cream, I always want to eat ice cream.

—Well, if your mom does not mind, I can invite you when we finish with this delicious cake, you see, the cart is there.

—Yes, yes, right, mom?

—He just bought it, there is nothing he likes more, but you are busy, and we are wasting your time, what will your family say?

—No, do not worry, it is just me and my son and he is spending time together with his friends and —God knows what time he will arrive. Rather, I have not asked about your husband.

—Jesus' father is in Spain, he has another family, we separated two years ago, and he remarried when we came to Paris.

From that moment Jean and Camille realized that they had found each other to start a new adventure together, from that day they waited for the moment to meet in the park to share food, wine, and the company of Jesus, who from the first moment found in man a great friend.

Chapter 28

Architecture Without Borders. The Colombian Women

Carolina is a Colombian architect older than Jean, she was on the island when the boy was still a student and they coincided in several events, the woman found the young man attractive and nice from the first moment, then, when they exchanged more, she realized that he was very intelligent and with a vision of design and architecture that somehow reminded him of his interests when he was a student. They have stayed connected for a couple of years and when she found out that he would arrive in Paris she at once wanted to be in contact with him. She has invited him to a meeting of the gestating movement "Architecture without Borders" in Andalusia and the young man, knowing that his mother lives in Spain, has accepted, so they prepare to make the trip by train.

The trip takes approximately 12 or 13 hours from Paris to Madrid, enough time for young people to talk about things that interest them. For Carolina, more than enough to see if the young man pays attention to her a little more, because until now he has not presented any other interest than the professional one and only talks about issues related to architecture, her projects and now those without borders. They must make a stopover in Barcelona and change trains, a place that Jean has always wanted to visit, so they spend hours there before continuing their journey.

Young people walk from the Barcelona Sant's train station to get to the famous Joan Miró Park, where the well-known woman and bird statue is. These square crosses the Gran Vía de las Cortes

Catalanas, one of the most important streets in the city. Jean takes photos and films, which for him is a dream come true. Carolina has been traveling the route times and only enjoys watching the young man's enthusiasm, who seems only interested in buildings, avoiding all his insinuations.

—Jean, we must eat something, it has been more than six hours since we had coffee on the train.

—Right away, I would like to take advantage of the little time we have until the other train.

—"Well, keep taking your photos and I'll buy something for the two of us at the corner cafeteria," —she said with the idea that he wanted to go with her, but he was not interested and just continued to focus on what he was doing without looking at her.

She walked away from him a bit angry and wondering what it was that kept Jean from realizing that he liked her and that she expected to see interest on her. The Colombian knew that she was a beautiful woman with a body worked on with exercises, which from an early age instilled in her the use of a girdle so that her waist would mark, and she would not accumulate fat in her stomach. She keeps a daily exercise routine and a meticulous diet by counting the calories that she consumes and not letting her mind make her eat sweet foods, because she knows that sweets have always been her temptation.

Finally, the young woman makes up her mind and buys chocolate and churros, because she is the easiest to have a good relationship with and because she cannot help but eat them every time, she finds a place had sold them. She approaches the young man who absorbed in his observation of the place:

—Look, Jean, I bought these churros you are going to like.

—Oh, thanks, yes sweet things really fascinate me.

—Me too, look at what we have in common.

—Everyone likes sweets.

—There are those who prefer salty or spicy things more than sweet.

—It could be, they buy me with any candy.

—I am lucky. "Since we left you haven't looked me directly in the face, even once," she says —He pretending to enjoy the food, walks away to look at a sign in the park.

—Well, I am going to sit down because I eat this once every thousand years, I should enjoy it.

She did not insist any more on extracting the young man and when the time came, they returned to the station to take the train that would finally take them to Madrid.

Chapter 29

The Reunion with Blanca in Madrid

A month has passed since Jean learned of her mother's fate, Blanca has invited him to come to Madrid and spend days with her, so before arriving in Andalusia he and Carolina came to see her. The woman received them with great affection and prepared food for them and she has a room ready for them to rest. At the end of dinner, they talk with Paco while his mother prepares coffee.

—So, do you want to go to the meeting this weekend?

—Yes, it is Saturday because other people cannot travel earlier due to work and other commitments.

—And where do the others come from?

—I imagine that fundamentally from other parts of Spain and the rest of Europe, although I know that there are other Africans – answers Carolina.

—That is a beautiful project, surely the most demanding thing is to find the financial means to carry it out.

—I really think it will be the biggest obstacle to overcome, but Jean has ideas so they will surely receive support, among others.

—Yes, what is it about? I mean yes, it is not complicated to explain to someone like me that —I only went to primary school.

—No, not at all, the good thing about it is that it is within the reach of people like you say who do not have education, because the collaboration of all the interested parties needed and especially of those who live in places with need. Explain to him, Jean.

—Well, I do not know if you know about the cooperatives created to work the land in places where the peasants do not have the resources to buy the products to cultivate, or the equipment.

Yes. Something like the agricultural communes?

—Exactly, in this case it would be to improve the habitat depending on the needs of the various places, it would be about improving not only the house but also the streets, park, and other parts of the urban environment.

—It sounds like an interesting millet, but those things cost money.

—Part of the idea is that the same people can work on the constructions in their spare time.

—As I say, I find it interesting and I hope they receive the necessary support, but, in any case, I think they will need financial support.

—What do you talk about politics? —Blanca enters with coffee cups.

—Not what Jean thinks about the group that they are forming in Andalusia.

—But *mijo*, don't you think you still have other things to resolve with your father about all that of the inheritance and the name?

—Yes, but in any case, we are here, and it seems interesting to me to start communicating with them. God! How long we can it take with the inheritance papers? I imagine that there are relatives who are not pleased that we just appeared.

—Do not tell me? You know, I imagine that the family never imagined that you existed, just as neither you nor your father would ever imagine that they would have a family in Paris. But also remember, I am a Spanish citizen, and you can also adopt my citizenship whenever you want.

—My dad is very excited about everything related to the surname, he is not very interested in the inheritance thing, he says that he has lived his whole life from his job but knowing about the family that he did not know existed on this continent, is something that has filled him with a lot of vitality and even a lover has found himself in Paris.

—That is incredibly good news, your dad is a good man, and he deserves to have a woman by his side who loves him and makes him happy.

—She is divorced, and she has a son with a special condition, she is in a wheelchair.

—She must be a special woman too.

—You will know her, we can come at any time, we just must wait for the papers to resolved and everything related to her last name to obtain French citizenship.

That night Blanca prepared a room for Jean and Carolina, since she had the idea that they were a couple. Seeing that Carolina said nothing, the young man approached her mother:

—Can you bring me blankets to stay on the sofa in the living room, please?

—It is that I prepared the other room for you, you will be comfortable there, the bed is big, and it is very fresh.

—Yes, Carolina is going to stay there, I can sleep here without problems.

—What, are you upset?

—The thing is ...

—Do not pay attention to him, ma'am, I will make sure he comes here.

Blanca leaves smiling and Carolina approaches Jean:

—You are not going to sleep here if there is a comfortable and big bed there, there's room for both, I promise I am not going to hurt you... she goes to the room between naughty laughter.

The young man follows her, she takes off her robe that covers a short green nightgown with strappy sleeves, very loose, comfortable, and fresh, a silk that clings to the body with movement and lets the young man appreciate her beautiful figure. the young woman, who has exercised all her life to support firm breasts along with a flat stomach. Jean's eyes run over Carolina's body, looking at her shapely legs, shiny from the cream she has put on. She lies on her back and looks at him:

—Come closer, you see, we can both sleep here without any problem, if you want, we can leave the window open and we can see the stars from the bed.

Jean goes into the sheets. She continues talking about the sky that they see through the window and slowly approaches him and kisses him calmly, as if they knew that it was the next step to take, inevitable, because she goes crazy for the man she has wanted since the first time she saw him in the island, and him because seeing the half-naked young woman has fervently desired her, although in his mind he knows that what is about to happen would change their relationship as colleagues, but without knowing that it would take him down an unexpected and unbridled path that would not be easy for him avoid.

Chapter 30

Andalusia

The weekend has finally arrived and Jean travels with Carolina to Andalusia, where her friends are waiting for them to take them to the place where the architects who have come to participates in the configuration of the organization they are forming, with the that intend to help poor communities in carrying out housing and community projects so that they can improve their quality of life.

They enter the hall of the Sevilla hotel, in the city of the same name, and there are about thirty people standing up greeting each other with commotion, Jean glances quickly to find himself in a corner, when a major surprise, there she is, Carmen. She is with her back to him talking to another architect, but he recognizes that figure wherever she is, it is her, who was his teacher and for whom he has that feeling from the first day he saw her. He approaches slowly and almost whispering in her ear:

—Professor.

She turns and almost loses her balance in astonishment:

—Jean, what are you doing here?

—I am asking the, a friend has invited me, and I have traveled with her from Paris.

Carolina with a loud laugh arrives where they:

—Carmen, I did not know you would come; someone had told me that they were trying to contact you but that you had not returned their emails.

—It is just that I was doing a job outside the faculty and until a couple of weeks ago I was able to respond, and you know running to be able to come, it is not easy for budgets to be approve from one moment to the next.

—How nice that you could come, your experience is very necessary in this type of project!

Jean just watches and listens, he has no intention of interrupting the conversation between the two women, for him the presence of the architect is the most surprise, but pleasant that he could have had. Being with her in a place outside the school, the rest of the students and teachers who prevented him from getting so close to her and who intimidated her so that they could see him as a man and not as a student. It is a play of fate that he could never imagine.

The meeting begins and the special guests for the occasion seated at a table where their names are mark, and the agenda and other important papers are in a folder appointed for them. The others are sitting on chairs around, Jean as he has come without an invitation, only going with Carolina, sits in one of the chairs outside the table, but placed right in front of Carmen, so they constantly exchange looks and smiles. Carolina is sitting in front of Jean, and she cannot see his face, but she can see the teacher's constant stares, which annoys her.

When the meeting ends, Jean approaches Carmen:

—Carmen, where are you staying?

—Here, in this very hotel.

—So do we, but we are going back to Madrid tomorrow and from there to Paris, I still have unfinished business there.

—I am also going to London tomorrow; I am going to teach a class and from there I return to the island.

—We only have one night.

—How for what?

—We can go out to the hotel garden later; they say that the bar is particularly good and that the Sevillian music is happy.

—Well, I arrive there at about nine.

She leaves and he goes to the hall when Carolina intercepts him:

—And? What does she say about the island?

—Nothing, we do not talk about that.

—And how much did they talk about?

—Nothing that interests you — he says annoyed.

—Well, do not be like that, if you want, we can have few drinks and relax, we can go somewhere for a while...

—No, I will be busy tonight, if you want you can go with your friends, I heard you were making plans...

—Are you not going to be with me?

—No, I have arranged to meet Carmen and we have things to talk about. I would rather we were alone. Anyway, you and I are going to Madrid tomorrow and we will have time to exchange impressions of today's meeting.

—But I am not interested in talking about the meeting, I just want to be with her.

—But today you cannot.

The young man leaves without another word, and she follows him in annoyance towards the room they share. He quickly goes to the bathroom and the young woman pours herself a glass of wine and stands on the balcony from where she, by chance, can see Carmen's room across the inner courtyard. There is the architect moving from one side to another as if she were choosing clothes. Carolina sulkily returns to the room as Jean leaves the bathroom, runs, and hugs him and starts kissing him, he separates her from him:

—Carolina, what are you doing?

—I kiss you. Do you like my kisses?

—Your kisses are fine, but I think we should talk, what happened last night does not mean that we have a relationship, I carried away for the moment, but you know that I really see you as a friend, an incredibly good friend, but nothing more, I love another woman.

—Yes, Carmen, right?

—I do not have to answer that, it is my private life, and I would appreciate it if you did not interfere, yesterday was a mistake, I should not have carried away, I do not want our friendship lost for a night of intimacy.

—But I love you, and not precisely as a friend.

—Forgive me, I cannot reciprocate that feeling because I love someone else.

She leaves the room annoyed, expecting him to follow her, but he does not, he finishes getting ready and goes on a date with the woman he loves. Carolina follows him without the young man noticing her and she sees him go to the garden where he meets Carmen who is beautiful in a black dress fitted to her figure, her hair loose and a natural rose in her hair. He approaches her and takes her by the waist, giving her a kiss on the cheek and together they sit near the dance floor where couple's dances to the soft rhythmic music played by the musicians.

The atmosphere of the patio is very romantic and at each table there are obviously couples having intimate moments, at the bar Carolina hides so as not to seen by Jean and Carmen who have sat near the musicians and drink wine. She notices that he has his arm around the woman's shoulders and seems to say something in her ear, then he sees them kiss. She is unaware that it is the first time that Jean kisses the teacher and that the couple is letting go of a mutual feeling that they have controlled for a long time.

She sees them dance close together and then leave for the elevator that goes to the rooms on the other side of the patio, where Carmen is staying. She follows them without them noticing and she sees them enter the room, then she goes to the opposite side to see the window closed and the lights go out.

Chapter 31

The Eternal Night

Carmen and Jean for the first time have carried away by the uncontrollable desire to be together and overflow the love they have. She has brought him to her room and entering they have merged in a warm kiss that have no end. He presses her on his chest, and she hardly has the strength to hold her arms around him, then they walk together to the edge of the bed and the young man tries to say something, she kisses him and prevents him from saying a word.

–You do not know how I have wanted this moment, since the first day I saw you walking through the corridors of the faculty, that day I fell in love with you, and I could not get you out of my mind.

–Let us not talk, I do not want to say something I will regret later, just kiss me and let me go crazy with you tonight, it is our night, and I do not know if we will ever have another time like this.

–Carmen –the young man tries to speak, but she stops him again.

The night passes slowly, and the lovers discover unknown sensations for them until that moment. They wish that the hours would not pass, and that the darkness would never give way to the light of day; they know that they only have that night, because at dawn each one will take a different course.

Jean has dreamed of this moment countless times, without being sure that it would ever come. Carmen, although she wanted it too, she never thought it would happen, in her mind there have been reasons to avoid it, but there they are, for the first time letting themselves carried away by love and the passion that consumes them, without thinking, just loving each other.

The first light of dawn surprises them, still wrapped in passion and ecstatic, staring into each other's eyes, as if they wanted to see the other's soul. She breaks the silence:

—You must go, I must prepare myself. They will come for me to take me to the airport. I would not want them to find you here.

—I do not want to separate from you.

—We must do it, remember that we must follow our paths, directions that take us to separate places.

—Yes, but we can fix that, you can come to Paris.

—You know I cannot, I must return to the island, and you still do not know how long everything can take you.

—I cannot lose you again, not now that I know you love me like I love you.

—I did not say I love you.

—I do and I cannot shut him up anymore.

—Let us leave it like that, I am still older than you, and besides, you already know that I have never been interested in having an emotional commitment.

—But Carmen...

—I tell you, let us leave it like that...

The young man gets up and prepares to leave her, looks at her and says:

—I will be on the patio at 9 in the morning, before leaving. If you want to find a way for us to be together, I will wait for you there.

Chapter 32

Fate Against Them Again

Jean keeps the taste of Carmen's kisses and the sensation of pleasure that he had having sex with her for the first time, he walks to her room knowing that she may not appear on the patio that morning. He opens the door of the room he shares with Carolina and to his surprise he finds her lying unconscious on the floor, he calls her and tries to wake her up, but he can't, then he realizes that she has a bottle in her hand, takes it and reads that they are relaxing pills, desperate he picks up the phone and calls the folder to ask for help.

He returns to the woman's body and notices that she is still breathing, at that moment two men enter the room and separate him to find the woman, then the paramedics enter with a stretcher and take her away. A man approaches him and asks who he is.

—I am a friend who travels with her, we came to a meeting and today we must return to Madrid, then to Paris where I have unfinished business next week.

—Look now you are not going to leave the room until I tell you, sit in that chair while I take photos and fingerprints. Look, have you read this paper?

—No, just saw her on the floor, and I have done nothing but ask for help.

—Who is Jean?

—I am.

—This is for you.

—For me? What does she say?

The man reads:

— "Jean, my love, I cannot bear the idea that you are with another woman after having spent unforgettable moments, in which you showed me how much you love me, I leave the way free for you, I am leaving, I hope you are happy"

Jean just covers his face with his hands and bewilderedly says:

—I do not understand, Carolina and I are just friends and I never thought she was capable of something like that, I am confused.

—I must tell you that you will have to go with me to the hospital to find out the status of your friend and then to the delegation so that you can give a statement. I hope there are no major complications, and the lady recovers from the episode soon, meanwhile we will detain you while we find out what happened. Where were you during the early morning?

—I was with a friend in another room.

It is possible that we must corroborate that, can you tell me which room and the name of the person?

—I would rather keep that a secret for now.

—It is your right, but if the case gets complicated you will have to tell us.

Jean and the inspector leave the hotel for the hospital. It is 9 am. On the patio, Carmen walks slowly towards the bar, looking around.

—Carmen, we only have ten minutes, if we take longer, you may miss your flight.

—Just give me a moment, I am waiting for someone...

She stands looking at the exit of the elevators, but she does not see him arrive, she looks at her watch and at the man who insists that they must leave, it is 9 and 10 minutes, he has not arrived.

She takes her bag from her and walks towards the exit, stops, and looks once more towards the bar. She passes a car with black windows and crosses the street to catch the waiting taxi.

From the car Jean sees her standing looking into the hotel, he tries to make a gesture, but her back is turn, she cannot see him.

Chapter 33

Jean at The Police Station

The inspector and Jean have been to the hospital and have informed that Carolina is unconscious and that they still do not know the consequences that she may have for having taken about 20 Lorazepam pills, a medication for depression, which helps to balance the chemical substances in the brain and insomnia. According to the doctor, the woman will be unconscious for about 24 hours, so the young man will have to wait at the police station until he can give a statement and all suspicions about him cleared up.

Hours have passed and the commissioner takes the young man to a small cell where there is an obviously drunk man who looks at him and points to a cot in front of him:

—Lie down there, a long night awaits us – he says with an accent that implies that he is not Spanish – it is already night, and the cells do not open again until morning.

—You have been here other times; I see that you are an expert in the matter – he tells him mockingly.

—I have been in all the police stations of the Mediterranean, in Europe and Africa – says the man also mockingly.

—But you are not Spanish...

—No, I am Moroccan, they call me Moor. You are not Spanish either...

—No, neither I am a Caribbean islander.

—Few years ago, in Morocco I met a woman who spoke like you, and they called her "La Isleña", she was a close friend of a woman I loved.

—My mother lived over there; they call her that.

It would be a lot of coincidence that it is the same, I went back to look for her to the place where she was, but she was gone, she and her friend wanted to escape from a place where they were kept almost as slaves, but the friend died, and I don't know what happened to her.

—It is no coincidence that we are talking about the same person, because my mother had to escape from a place like that and she also had a Spanish friend who died.

—So if it is her, fate has brought us together, because I have wanted to see her because I have an outstanding debt with her and, furthermore, there is money that María Elena had given me to bring him to Spain and give it to him when they arrived, she was afraid of having so much money with her because she didn't know if they discovered it, they could even kill her.

—But how come you could not help the islander?

—Bad luck, in one of my drunken sprees they arrested me for a fight and when I went back to look for her, she was not there, nobody knew how she had left, because she left no trace, everything was intact, the only thing missing in the room was a small TV that was always on.

The next day, both men were able to go out and already on the street, Jean showed the Moor a photograph he had of his mother, realizing that it was the same woman, the Moroccan almost jumped with happiness, because he was worried that he was going to look bad with his friend whom he had loved very much.

Chapter 34

The Reunion of The Moor and The Isleña

Jean and El Moro have picked up Carolina who has recovered, although with medical recommendations to control her anxiety and depression. Jean is worried and wants to get her back to Paris as soon as possible so she can see the doctor who is treating her. They travel in the van in which the Moor moves around Europe, he goes from country to country in a nomadic way, he only has the front seat, in which the three of them fit, and in the back, he has countless things, which not even the same can list.

The trip from Andalusia to Madrid is approximately six and a half hours, time that Jean will take advantage of to see the landscape and for Carolina to loosen up a bit, he is eager to be able to leave her at home and leave the episode of the night before behind, he thinks continually in Carmen, he left with the question of whether or not she came to see him in the hotel patio. He has no way of communicating with her, he will have to contact the architects who invited her to get information on how to reach her, that will take time.

The woman does not stop talking. The Moor turns up the volume of the radio to see if she can rest from her chatter, but this annoys Jean more than he just wants to think about his beloved, so he pretends to sleep leaning against the glass of the car window. They make a stop when they arrive in Córdoba to eat something and stretch their feet. The young man wants to see the Mosque-Cathedral, so he takes the opportunity to separate from his companions, entering the place.

Jean walks through the halls corroborating that really, as he had read, the place represents the crossbreeding of the city's character, the cathedral with the soul of a mosque with Umayyad, Gothic, Renaissance and Baroque styles; and most importantly, that the main altar coexists with a Mihrab or Muslim holy place, something that does not happen anywhere else. He enjoys looking at the jade and marble columns, the Byzantine mosaics framed in Renaissance naves. Read that this was the second most important temple in the Muslim world, only behind Mecca itself, and that it completed in the 10th century, that it would function as a Mosque until the reconquest in the 13th century, when it would use as a Cathedral after his consecration.

He lost in thought when he enters the "Patio de Los Naranjos," guarded by rows of orange and palm trees, horseshoe arches and the sound of fountains. He inevitably remembers the coffee plantation and Carmen. He walks slowly through the rows of trees thinking about the time he spent with his beloved, a feeling of loneliness encompasses him, and a tear runs down his cheek, while he tirelessly repeats the teacher's name. The Moor calls him and makes him come out of his daze. They return to the car to continue the journey.

Late at night they arrive in Madrid, where Blanca receives them astonished to see her son in the company of the Moor.

—What is this man doing with you?

—Let us explain, you will not believe what happened to us and where we met.

The incredulous woman, doubting the benefit of the meeting, tells them to come in. Paco has also joined them and perplexed, they listen to the story that the young man tells them.

—So that is why you did not show up when I expected you, because you were a prisoner Moro of hell.

—When I looked for you, you were already gone, and nobody knew how to tell me...

—And what did you do with my money?

—I kept the money that María Elena gave me for when you arrive in Spain, she was afraid that they would take it from you.

—What are you talking about? She did not tell me anything about other money.

—It is that she was afraid that they would know that she had more money than she intended to bring, you know how with things there, anyone could hurt them if they knew they brought more money.

—It is about sixty thousand dollars. I do not have them with me now because I did not know this was going to happen, but I swear woman, I have not touched it.

—I do not know if I believe you, when I see, it will be something else.

—Part of that money is for her brother, she explained to me that if something happened to her, it would divide between him and you.

Well – says Paco – now she and I are one.

—I see that, and I am glad because it is what the deceased would have wanted most.

They ended up making plans for the delivery of the money, the Moor promised to keep the word he gave his friend before he died.

...

Jean and Carolina have gone for a walk and the young man takes the opportunity to talk about the situation in which he was involved, due to the madness of the woman who took those pills.

—Carolina, do you have any idea about the trouble you got me into when they took me to the police station?

—I know, forgive me, it is just that I got a feeling of loneliness when I saw you with Carmen and saw them kiss together in her room.

—Are you spying on me?

—I just followed you.

—Look Carolina, the best thing is that you and I do not see each other for a while. You need to focus on your new job, and I already know that I have things ahead of me.

—But Jean...

—You know that I can be your friend, but nothing more.

—I know that you are interested in Carmen, but look, she left, and she did not care that they took you prisoner.

—We do not know that, besides, even if I do not see her again, I am only interested in you as her friend and so you do not get confused, it is best that we stop seeing each other.

—Jean, I am going to Colombia for a while before returning to Paris, you think that when I return, we could be friends again.

—I do not know Carolina, for now it is better that you go your way, and we do not see each other anymore.

Chapter 35

Jean Owner of Everything

Few months have passed, Jean and his father have achieved French nationality and named heirs to Madame Joubert's fortune. They installed in the apartment in Paris and hope to travel to the island soon. The architect wants to know the state of Los Naranjos and if there is any way to recover them. Sitting on the balcony, the young man and his father contemplate the sunset over the city and drink cognac. Jesús plays by hoisting one of his kites and Camille reads one of her poetry books sitting next to the architect's father.

—Mijo, how were we going to imagine this a couple of years ago when you wanted to study the Los Naranjos coffee plantation?

—My fate tied to that place, so I want to go back and find out if we can get it back. There were things there that intrigued me. That story of love and misfortune is also a family story. Did you know that the Frenchman's wife name was Carmen?

—Yes, you told me. I do not know whether to think it is a coincidence or fate, there is something inexplicable in that story.

—If you mean that Carmen and I can end up together, I don't know, nothing I've tried to contact her has worked for me, I don't know if she wants us to see each other again, the last time we agreed to see each other in a place, and —I can't know if it was because I ended up in a police station.

—If it is up to God that you will be together, nobody is going to be able to prevent it.

—Who knows, now that we return to the island, I will try to look for her.

Jean gets up and walks towards the railing to look at the street, his thoughts take him to the night he and his beloved Carmen danced and made love in Andalusia and he wonders if when he saw her leaving the hotel she was coming from the patio where he had to wait for her and terrible fear seized him, could it be that the teacher was looking for him that unfortunate morning? "I definitely have to go back to the island" he thinks, he turns and looking at his father says:

—Tomorrow, we will buy the tickets.

Why the rush? You are just sorting things out here, you still have unfinished business with your cousins and the lawyers.

—Do you know what we are going to do? You stay, you are the main heir.

Chapter 36

Back to Los Naranjos

September 22, 1992

Five years have passed since the first visit to the coffee plantation. This time they have better resources and with the experience of other jobs. They are no longer students; they want to create a tourist center in the mountains using the ruins of the place. Jean is another, he has traveled to Paris and has assumed French nationality. In Spain he met the architects without borders and talked to them about the place he wanted to rescue. He gets out of the car and asks: When do we leave?

—Carmen has not arrived.

—I did not know she was coming. Who contacted her?

—Impossible not to do it, the photos, the notes, and the sketches are hers, she never gave them to the institute – Answers Odalis.

—It does not matter; it is time for her and me to clarify things.

—What things?

—Our stuff.

Carmen arrives, she is radiant, with shorter hair and wide glasses that try to hide her black eyes. He smiles at her. She gives him her hand and Jean pulls her to him and kisses her on the cheek.

During the trip, Jean thinks that there is nothing he wants more than to rescue Los Naranjos. He has become his great obsession, although he does not do anything else in his life, he wants that place to last and keep the memory of Carmen and the

Frenchman forever. They pass through the town and reach the causeway, nothing has changed. The cliff, the top and the precipice, where you stop to contemplate the sky that blends with the coffee plantations and the smell of orange. The dense fog prevents them from seeing the valley, so they decide to continue walking and arrive at the *bohio*. There is no one there. At last, the old gate, behind nothing, few remains of wood and stones everywhere, tiles, twisted iron. Where is the hipped tile roof? The staircase, the balcony, the garden fountain. Everything has disappeared. They cry.

They approach the Batey where Lucia is waiting for them, dressed in those striking colors that characterize her.

–How sad to see that everything is in ruins, nobody informed us of the situation of this place – says Jean – there is nothing to do.

–Sadly, it is like that, the misfortune of the rains and the hurricane ended everything, we could barely survive and save what we have, the crop failed, and we have only been able to survive thanks to the will of these peasants who do not want to leave these lands.

The sadness has sown the pain of loss in everyone, because without any reason each one retires somewhere to contemplate what they considered already part of them as well. Carmen approaches Lucia and asks her:

–How are you? I found out that Marianela left the Batey. I can imagine how you must feel.

–Yes, she decided to look for life outside this place and when she writes to me, she always tells me that this is her land but that here she would never be herself. Look, this was the first letter he sent me – Carmen takes the paper and reads:

—This is the story of what happened before my departure. I write it to you my Maita, from the depths of my heart:

—"The land seemed empty to me as I ran through the trees and ferns on the damp hill that hid the old Batey house. I always enjoyed running through the small bushes and the green grass of the thickets, seeing the peasants who slept with their women at any time of the day, or at night, because they could not resist the primitive desire to have a sweaty and animal sex while they waited for the rain to stop, or for the mud to harden to continue the work.

—I heard the stories of pregnant women with fatherless children, and they created in me the rejection of the idea of giving herself to any man, because I feared being part of the common statistic. You know that I am distrustful, and it was difficult for me to show my beauty, that wild beauty that made me strike in the eyes of any man. My dry and coarse speech, riding a horse with a shirt and tall boots, trying to hide my femininity, turned me into just another peasant with whom the workers shared their stories of conquests and loves in the town and what is the most desired woman for the next dance.

—You know that I never attended the dances, I worked and took care of the animals in the farmyard. The remaining time was reading, reading was what he most wanted to do. I read everything that fell into my hands, which is why the neighbors often consulted me, because they said that surely "I had read about it." They respected me, yes, they respected and admired me. You know the women of the town only give birth and raise boys; they did not understand that dancing was not only what was in the *batey*. I knew that there was another dance called Ballet, although I had never seen it. He knew that beyond the limits of the town there was another world where there were things about which he had learned.

—The only people she could talk to would be the teacher and the nurse, but they were not always in town. The women in the family, you know, only talked about winning over their husbands to take them shopping. What I wanted most was to be able to see the ballet, to see that dancer who appeared in the magazines standing on pointe, like the one she had hanging in my room. Before sleeping she was the image that always remained in my eyes. Sometimes, I imagined that I am myself a dancer.

—That day in the farmhouse I saw the announcement that dancers were coming and would give a performance in the ballroom. The ballet had come to me. I got to the ballroom early and saw the dancers lifting a young girl, but she had no slippers, no feathers on her tutu. All day I was watching the rehearsal and there I stayed quiet, speechless until the room filled, the music sounded, and the function began. Then the lights went out, and they all went to the Batey and the rum. I only imagined myself in the center of the stage. Suddenly, someone walked towards me. It was the one not wearing a tutu, the one who had danced that night. She came with a tall, corpulent man, also a dancer.

—There, in the same room, we talked about contemporary dance, and I knew that the company would stay in the houses of the community, because there was no hotel in the town to stay. I invited her to come to my house. We left and from the house we listened to the music of the dance and for the first time someone told me about the things I wanted to know about the city, about what I imagined and had never seen.

—The dancers visited all the nearby villages for a week. The other young man was at my Aunt Lula's house, and they went to the village early. At night we went back to talks about things we should know and experience. They danced for me and taught me things of which I had never heard. They showed me a world that seemed more fascinating to me every day.

—The last show arrived, after rehearsal in the morning we went to the river and enjoyed the turns in the water, and the waterfall. They asked me to go to the city with them, that I was incredibly young and that they would help me follow my dream of being a dancer.

—I did not think about it and when they left, I also got on the bus and left. I know it must have hurt you and times you will wonder how I am. I can only tell you that I am happy, with them I learned about dancing, they taught me and took me to see the world. Now I am a different person."

—She is happy— Carmen tells Lucia – I am glad that she was not afraid, and she followed what her heart desired.

—Yes, I am sad because she was my sun and my company, but also when I read her letters, I know that she did the best for her, and in the end she did not live through the destruction of Los Naranjos, she loved this place and the house was the place where she played all her games as a child, the river, the spring were her favorite places.

—Mine too Lucia, this place stood for a great illusion for me, to be able to help reconstruct a fascinating story and give Los Naranjos a new air of happiness in the middle of this paradise.

The important thing is that you and the other are here now, and you have given us boundless joy, knowing that they did not forget about us.

—Look, Lucia, I brought you photos from when we came the first time, it is a memory, look at the mansion so you can also send it to Marianela.

Chapter 37

Andrew's Secret

Odalis and Clara walk through the old town towards the store, looking for food and rum for that last day when they would say goodbye to Los Naranjos. The others have kept each to their own, but Odalis wants to hear the story from her friend's lips, because they have all been friends since the first day they met at the university and although they no longer live close to each other, their friendship has not diminished.

Clara begins the narration:

–There is no doubt, it was Andrés who was humming a song in front of my door. After five years he greeted the friend. There was my Adonis, with whom I had dreamed in my adolescence, my employer to conquer. When we greeted each other, my lips brushed the collar of his shirt and there stayed the usual mark of lipstick that we used to fight over when we were young. His chest less marked than before, shaved, and the hairy arms that I loved, now tattooed. The hair on his forehead was gone and two large receding hairlines marked maturity. We talked nonstop, as always, telling me about his life, the new truths about him, and others that I did not learn until later.

The meeting began with jokes and anecdotes from the past. We ate. And the unexpected questions and answers began. – "Andrés, what happened to your marriage?"

–You know we moved just married and expecting a child. At that stage it was just working and taking care of the baby. In the country there is not much to do. There we lived alone, and we did not notice that each one did what he wanted, nobody criticized us, nor did they notice what was or was not different. Returning to my parents' house already started the other story, we were not alone, there were others seeing and sharing the same space. She was doing the specialty and she met a patient with whom she fell in love. She told me that they had not had relations, but that it would happen soon, so she decided to leave and take the child.

—Are they still together?

—Yes, and they are very well.

—And the boy?

—He is with me. The truth is, she is not particularly good at motherhood. She takes him out on the weekends sometimes, but he is with my family about 80 percent of the time.

The inevitable debate ensued, and the topic of infidelity covered the air. We ended with an anonymous survey of how of those present had been inclined to be unfaithful at a point. When collecting the ballots, half of those present had thought about it. I found it curious that we knew each other more than ten years ago and I had never asked myself if any of my university classmates had been unfaithful to their partners, since we were all in the same group and they had been together long before letting us start the race.

Reading the results, the atmosphere changed. No one expressed alarm, decided to leave, sensing that, as the night progressed, other hidden things would become known. What began anonymously could become revealed. I was not interested in knowing who each ballot belonged to, but others overwhelmed by intrigue and began the investigation.

I must admit that at first the conversation was not to my liking, the idea of meeting was to remember old times, have an enjoyable time and know what we had done in those years in relation to what we had studied. Good and a little bit of gossip, but without bad intentions. Now I realize that life takes us down paths sometimes unimagined, and reconnecting with friends means accepting friends as they are and not as we want or wish they were.

Few months before, when I told Andrés that he wanted us to get together and look for the others, I did not imagine that the situation would be a little more uncomfortable for him because everyone would ask about what happened in his marriage. After graduating, each of us went to his place of origin and us were already engaged or in a couple, he got married just after graduating. The others either stayed with the same partner or looked for another, in my case, a couple of divorces.

With the passing of the night and the drinks, new veils were falling, and the realities of each one surprised the other, from those who have not worked in anything like what they studied, or those who changed their minds about religion or politics. As the experience of being mothers or fathers has changed their lives, and other needs change due to age. In the end, Andrés, after drinks, began to talk about his own changes:

–Religion has always seemed fascinating to me and with the changes in married life I got close to the Jesuit community that is close to my house, there I got involved in the studies they gave and over time I became interested in the life I was leading, the difficulty was my son, Andresito. Seeing that my interest was real, they suggested that I give the child up for adoption to my parents so that I could freely enter the seminary. Sure, no sign It means that I have completely neglected my son, but you know my mom always loved him as her own and anyway she also spends time with Silvia. In addition, my dad took it and brought it with me when I was a child, you know that he loves sports, especially going swimming. Now here you see me, shortly: "Your friend the priest." How about?

Odalis, who has listened to the story silently, smiles and says:

—I'm glad, I knew he wouldn't be happy with Silvia, she always gave me the impression that she was looking beyond the life they had together, on my visits to her house, she left us alone and went to the room under the pretext about the baby, but I knew it was because he wasn't very interested in things about him. Now, what a good doctor she is, that cannot deny, people loved her because she dedicated time to patients, and at whatever time it was.

They arrive at the store and choose things for the evening meeting, where they have invited the peasants who helped them so much and whom they may never see again. On the way back they continue the talk, and this time Odalis asks Clara:

—Tell me about your parents, after they moved from the city, we already lost contact, I found out that your father died.

—If the old man left shortly after we moved, the treatment did not work as we expected and, in a heartbeat, he left us. My mother was devastated, and I oversaw her. Fortunately, a friend of hers brought a priest to the house who had studied psychology and, together with her experience and my mother's faith, I managed to get her through. Since then, she has been involved in the things of the parish, she helps as a catechist and she feels useful, imagine that there was a time when she wanted me to become a nun

—Ahhhhaaa, the other cannot help laughing.

—Yes, and he sent the nuns to the house to convince me, the good thing is that I met Joaquín who played the organ, and first because —I asked him to help me get my mom and the nuns off me, and then because really, we fell in love, I was able to free myself from that torment. —I think I rushed into that marriage, because sometimes we divorced after a year, but I freed myself from the torture of the nuns, then I remarried and, in any case, I still haven't found the man who understands me and lets me be sculpted with calm down, they don't understand why I spend hours observing and drawing what they call "those little things you do".

–It is that your miniature sculptures are complex, times you must see them with a magnifying glass.

–That is why I also work with magnifying glasses. It is complicated, but for me it is the realization of what I have always wanted to be.

–Friend, I am happy for you, you know that I have always loved you very much and I know how hard you will work to graduate, even if you want to do something else.

–Yes friends, look, in the end we return to this place and what we imagined for a long time has turned to dust. But we have a friendship.

Chapter 38

Los Naranjos Forever

Los Naranjos, September 23, 1992

Everyone has gathered on the esplanade where the house was and they have improvised a fire, Carmen has brought her guitar and the young people have prepared meat and food with the help of the women from the *batey*. Peasants have joined them and tell what has happened in the last two years, how the waters and the cyclone devastated the area, how they evacuated and taken to a nearby town, and when they returned there was nothing.

—It is sad to lose everything – comments Carmen – they had to begin from nothing.

—Well, the authorities helped us, but the truth is that we did the biggest job here, we cut down trees, built new huts, fixed the course of the river, because it overflowed and covered the orange and coffee plantations, we had to start preparing the land full of a weed that grew in a matter of days on dead coffee plants.

—It sounds terrible, and I imagine that the animals died.

—You cannot imagine, they were lying everywhere, and their rotten bodies gave off an odor that not one could resist. Peasants who did not want to evacuate also died. Often, people are very stubborn.

—The sad thing is that there is nothing left, it is as if they had swept away the place, as if the earth swallowed everything there was.

—Imagine that the waters went down the mountain's kilometers and kilometers below, also the overflowing river took what in its path to the coast.

—Too bad, but well today we are here remembering our first visit and remembering those who are no longer here.

—Old Ramon until the end hope to see you return because he said that young Jean would come to build the coffee plantation again.

—I am so sorry, we have been a bit late, but here we are, even if it is just to remind you.

—And Juan, who kept his word to take care of the house until he died, one day he came to say goodbye, he said that he was going to rest, and we do not know where he went, he never came back.

—That is life, old people are leaving, one day it will be our turn too.

The afternoon falls between music, food and rum, the farewell of a chapter in the lives of the students and Carmen, the teacher. The story of a coffee plantation, its people and a batey that they will never forget. Gathered around the campfire, they sing old songs, laugh at college anecdotes and the things they cannot forget about the first time they were in the coffee plantation.

An atmosphere of nostalgia and joy at the same time surrounds them, everyone finally accepted the disappearance of Los Naranjos. The peasants begin to withdraw and only the former students remain, they insist on the afternoon being longer, because they know that it is the last time, they will see the sun set between the mountains of that place. The reddish sky and the smell of coffee drying are the perfect touch to keep that day in the memory. The last drinks of the rum that they sell in the town store and the jerky that the *guajiras* brought to share, a bit of *hayacas*, yucca and *congrí* are part of the dinner that they have left to end the evening.

No one wants to admit that the afternoon is passing away and they still are together until the last of the campfire extinguished. The day is over and so is the adventure.

Chapter 39

The End

Night has fallen and the crickets sing, the smell of Jasmine surrounds them and curled up in a blanket they look at the starry sky. In the distance the sound of drums. Jean gets up and walks to the river. The moon shines on the water and the current seems to play a sad melody. Carmen follows him and sits next to her.

—I fell in love with this place, the first time.

—You do not believe in love.

—It is true.

—In France I just wanted to come back here and sometimes I dreamed that you were with me.

—Yes, I thought about the Frenchman, his wife, coincidences, orange trees, and love.

Jean looks at her and she smiles.

—I told you would smile at me in Los Naranjos.

Jean hugs her and kisses her, she feels for the first time that she can love him without fear and abandons herself to the experience. The rooster crows, the mockingbirds flutter over the orange blossoms and the silhouette of the mountain shimmers in the light of the rising sun. Lovers know that Paris awaits them, the city from where Jean Joubert traveled to the coffee plantation with his wife Carmen. Los Naranjos has died, but the love between the French and the Spanish lives on.

Pencil Notes: Los Naranjos

The famous Voltaire (1694-1778), an illustrious man of philosophical thought, mocked the doctors who discouraged coffee, saying "If coffee is a poison, it must be very slow: "I have been drinking it for eighty years and I have not died yet". In another, a diligent servant assiduously served a foaming and steaming cup of the "black nectar of the gods" to Victor Hugo (1882-1885) during the feverish process of writing his maximum work "Les Misérables". Coffee has shaped the taste of hundreds of historical celebrities and the deep social fabric of multitudes in the synchronic and diachronic dimension of separate times and latitudes.

The Revolution, led by Toussaint L'Ouverture, at the end of the 18th century that took place in Haiti determined the mass flight of French residents in that country, along with part of their endowments of slaves and freedmen, to the island of Cuba, settling mainly in the mountainous strip of the Sierra Maestra and in the Nipe-Sagua-Baracoa Mountain range, territory that today is included in the provinces of Santiago de Cuba, Guantánamo, and Holguín.

At the dawn of the 19th century, successive waves of these immigrants promoted population and coffee settlements in the Guantánamo Basin, which ceased to be an uninhabited area to already have seventy-eight haciendas dedicated to this crop in 1819.

The first references to the Los Naranjos coffee plantation correspond to the year 1851, when Juan Bautista Chibás bought fifteen mainland caroes from Benjamín Starch, where he promoted the coffee plantation, which by then adjoined the Ermitaño, Joven María, Dios Ayuda and Monte Verde coffee plantations.

Los Naranjos was the most complete coffee agro-industrial complex in the Yateras region in Guantánamo, it had ten dryers, constituting the grain pulping base in the 19th century. In those dryers, on days of celebration and holidays, musical-dance values created or transmitted by slaves developed as part of the non-tangible heritage of Cuban culture, in the songs and dances of the "Tumba Francesa". In them, with refined elegance the men danced; the women coquettishly squandered Versailles charms, copied from the white wives, but seasoned with a certain Creole picaresque, suitable for the voluptuousness of African, Gallic, and Hispanic miscegenation.

In the ruins of the once splendid Los Naranjos hacienda, the old fermentation tanks preserved a section of the original channeled wall still survives, and the dam built, approximately six hundred meters from the house, continues today to supply the small town.

The manor house was a human wonder that appeared in the jewel of wild, virgin nature, the North American traveler Samuel Hazard described it as: the most beautiful place of all those I visited is the well-known Naranjal, found remarkably high in the mountains on a plateau and extending the cultivation in places not yet seen. It stands as a construction of non-Hispanic typology in the Caribbean, with two floors, the floors, made of different colored woods, have given it chromatic perspectives that enriched, along with the furniture, the living space. The 4-pitch roof, made of flat galvanized zinc, could be seeing from a distance, given the elevated position of the settlement; the fixed windows also offered the possibility of scanning the horizon and the confines of the property, while allowing the circulation of breezes.

The remains of funeral tombs in the form of mounds found in the cemetery, close to the dwelling house, denote their non-Hispanic characteristics.

From the “black shore”[1] of Cuba-Haiti- sciences and essences of our identity came to us, in 1895 the apostle of the independence of the green Antillean alligator, José Martí, left from Cap Haitian to Playita de Cajobabo to immolate himself in the "Necessary War". Martí loved and was love in the homeland of Dessalines.

At the end of the independence war in Cuba, the splendid coffee plantations left in ruins. Among the luxuriant green of the foliage, entangled with the foggy vapor of the clouds, in the vestiges of Los Naranjos there still survives some rosebush in flower, and like the rose of France today the cry of life sprouts in this short novel, by Salomón Leroux, brevity pregnant with reminiscences, esoteric coincidences, full of ideo-thematic plans, which barely pointed out make room for other stories, other cracks on the edge of the knife of subsistence.

In 2000 at the meeting of the UNESCO World Heritage Committee they declared a World Heritage Site, the coffee settlements registered with the name of Archaeological Landscape of the first coffee plantations in the southeast of Cuba. The ruins of Los Naranjos are a silent denunciation of the depredation, by action or indolence, of people to the history, culture, and heritage.

[1] Expression taken from a letter from José Martí to the Haitian poet Edmond Hereaux.

Los Naranjos Pictures

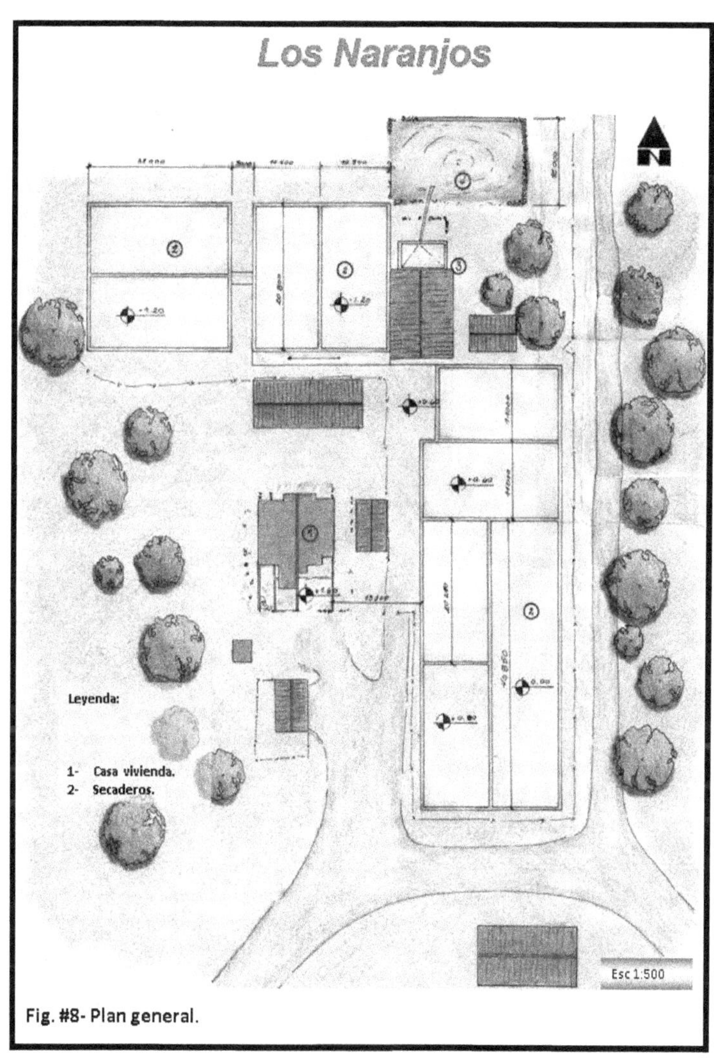

Fig. #8- Plan general.

Other Coffee Farms in Eastern Cuba

La Deseada

San Isidro

Bella Vista

Dios Ayuda

L'Ermitage

Contents

EDITORIAL PRIMIGENIOS
CORPUS LÍRICO DE UNA NACIÓN

www.ingramcontent.com/pod-product-compliance
Lightning Source LLC
LaVergne TN
LVHW010108170826
845678LV00012B/2294

* 9 7 9 8 8 1 9 5 1 7 9 7 0 *